BY HER MAJESTY'S COMMAND

UNVEILING THE BREXIT CONFLICT

NORBERT REICH

SWEETSPIRE LITERATURE
MANAGEMENT

For Kristian Peter, my son

I asked God for a best friend, he sent me my son.

Unknown

TABLE OF CONTENTS

CHAPTER I

BERLIN

He missed. The bullet only grazed the right temple of the President of the European Union and Chancellor of Germany leaving a small and superficial flesh wound. He thought about taking another shot but it was too late. The Chancellor had been pushed to the ground by his security forces, two of them lying on top of him covering his body. Now there was mayhem on Pariser Platz next to the Brandenburg Gate in Berlin. Thousands had gathered here to hear their chancellor speak in celebration of June 17, 1953, the day when the people of Germany had revolted against the communists only to be subdued by Russian tanks. Adam Bergman knew he had to leave quickly the room he had chosen at the Adlon Hotel. From here he had a clear view of the stage where the Chancellor of Germany was to address his countrymen. Now time was of the essence, he had to leave at once. Very soon the hotel would be cordoned off and swarming with security forces. There was no time to take along his favorite weapon, his Savage- Anschutz .223 sniper rifle. He threw it onto the bed and quickly left the room. The elevator was no longer a choice for his escape, so he ran down the stairs and stepped into the crowded lobby of the fashionable hotel. Now he slowed his pace and strolled toward the passageway to the right of the main entrance. Adam knew that leaving the hotel via the wide doors which led unto the main thoroughfare, Unter den Linden, would be a mistake. Surely this would be the way the Berlin police would enter the hotel. The passageway was short and lined by several boutique shops. Adam strolled leisurely glancing at the windows of the stores. Then he entered one of them, a gallery, at the end of the short passageway.

"Guten Tag," he said to the young lady attending the store.

"Guten Tag", was the reply.

"If I can help you answer questions, please do not hesitate to ask."

"Danke schoen," he replied, "I am just browsing, killing time while my wife is spending all my money." The attractive,young woman smiled in response.

Adam took a few minutes to survey the paintings and then exited the store through the door which led to Unter den Linden, Berlin's main thoroughfare, which to the west led to the Pariser Platz. But Adam walked in the other direction, east, towards Museum Island, one of Berlin's main attractions. The street was busy, people all now rushing towards the Brandenburg Gate to see what all the commotion was about. He saw the Bus 100 as it pulled into the bus stop only a few meters from him, and he entered the bus. Adam Bergman decided to take the bus to the Friedrich Strasse Ufer and take the tourist boat trip on the river Spree. After all he was just a tourist anxious to see all of Berlin's landmarks.

He bought a ticket at the small ticket van parked adjacent to the river and entered the boat of the Rederei, Stern & Kreis. The boat was almost completely occupied and Adam was the last person to step on board. He took one of the last seats on the deck of the tourist boat as it pulled away from its dockage. It was a beautiful day in mid-June, a blue sky, not a cloud above, and it was warmer than usual for this time in Berlin.

When the young waitress approached him Adam ordered a beer, a Berliner Kindl from Fass, a tap beer. Adam leaned back in his chair as the boat passed Berlin's Museum Island. He did not listen to the tourist guide describing all the landmarks. Adam reminisced.

CHAPTER II

CAPRI, ITALY

It had only been a few weeks ago when a man approached him as he and Nicole, his fiancée, were enjoying a cocktail on the terrace of the Quisisana Hotel on the island of Capri in Italy. Adam had decided to leave the assassination business. He was a trained killer groomed by the Navy Seals, the NSA, the national security agency in the United States, and by the Mossad, Israel's renowned intelligence agency. When Nicole Jefferson, a former CIA agent joined him, they became a formidable team in high demand. Their last assignment had been very lucrative and both had agreed it was time to let go. The island of Capri was now their home.

The man was clearly British, dressed in a dark blue suit, tie, stiff lips and a London accent. First, he had asked for directions to a restaurant on the island. Then he noticed the Daily Telegraph. A British newspaper opened to the sports page, resting on Adam's table.

"Are you a sports fan?" he asked awkwardly, hoping to begin a conversation.

"A fan?" Nicole responded. "He is not a fan, he is addicted to it. Never misses a game on television, no matter the hour."

"I am as well," the Brit responded. "My favorite team is Arsenal. What is yours?"

"I do watch the British Premier League, but I am a Bundesliga fan, and my favorite team is Bayern Munich."

"A world class team, one of the best in Europe. How do you think they will fare this year in the UEFA cup?"

"Of course, they will win," Adam said with a smile.

"Perhaps," the man responded, "but I am not sure of their new coach, are you?"

"Please", Adam interrupted, "have a seat and join us for a drink. I love to discuss soccer with knowledgeable fans."

"Well thank you," the Brit responded as he took a seat next to Adam on the terrace.

"But if you do not mind, I would prefer a cup of tea."

Both Nicole and Adam liked the man, he was personable, had a dry sense of humor and he knew soccer.

So when the Brit asked them to have dinner with him, they did not hesitate. Since the man did not know any of the restaurants, Adam suggested one of his favorite restaurants, Terrazza Brunella. All decided to meet at 8 p.m.

LONDON, ENGLAND, 10 DOWNING STREET

Margaret Sawyer, the new British Prime Minister, laid in her bed, she could not sleep. As a matter of fact she had not slept well for several months. It was only the sleeping pills that helped to get her some rest. It was her conscience that kept her awake. She had made a decision, one she knew was wrong, wrong for her people, the people of Britain. But she knew that the decision would get her to become only the second woman to be Prime Minister. She had allowed her ambitions to supersede what was best for her country.

The British people were almost equally divided on the issue of Brexit, whether Britain should leave the European Union. And when the former P.M., a staunch supporter to keep Britain in the EU, announced that he would resign if the people voted to leave the E.U, she saw her opportunity. Then Buckingham Palace had called. The Royal family wanted to have a chat with her, as the man on the phone had put it.

The meeting at the Palace was brief. Margaret Sawyer was instructed that her Majesty wanted Britain to leave the European Union. It was an embarrassment that Britain played only second fiddle in the European Union. Britain needed to once more become what it once had been, a world power, Europe's leader. To convince the British people Margaret was told to play on the pride of the people, on their belief of superiority, on the past. But officially she was to use a different explanation why the people should support Brexit, use the migration issue, she was instructed

There was no discussion, Margaret Sawyer was only allowed to listen. When she left the Palace and glanced back at the formidable building as the car took her back to her office, she wondered how thick the walls were. How much they were isolating the Royals from the real world. But she also knew that to become only the second woman to be Prime Minister of Great Britain she would do all she had been instructed to do at Buckingham Palace.

CHAPTER III

LONDON, ENGLAND, 85 ALBERT EMBANKMENT, VAUXHALL, LAMBETH

Theresa Watson sat in her spacious office overlooking the river Thames. Her office is located in the south western part of central London on the bank of the river Thames. It is decorated with contemporary furniture, but the chair she sat in was almost 100 years old. A swivel wooden chair her great grandfather had bought at the flea market when he was a student at Oxford University. It was all he had then possessed and it now was an heirloom to her. She slowly turned the chair to look out of her large window, to see the river Thames and Vauxhall bridge.

Theresa Watson is the head of the SIS, Secret Intelligence Service of Great Britain, or better known as MI6 (MI standing for Military Intelligence). This is the agency responsible for international intelligence. She assumed the office when her predecessor, a diplomat, resigned. Theresa was not a diplomat, but had been MI6's best field agent for almost 20 years.

As she looked at the Thames River and the Vauxhall bridge, she again shook her head in disbelief. Her people, the people of Britain, had voted to exit the European Union. She was convinced it was a mistake, a mistake which could ruin her country.

The current Prime Minister, Margaret Sawyer, had assured the British people it was the right thing to do, that Britain would flourish again, become once more a world power. She had promised that Britain would demand and receive special treatment from the EU, favorable trade agreements, acceptance of Britain's solution on the migrant issue and more. Promises only politicians have the audacity to make. Promises only a politician's conscience would allow. Theresa smiled at the thought. Theresa knew this was all but rhetoric, rhetoric to win votes. All would be different when negotiations finally took place behind closed doors, negotiations her country men would never be part of, never learn.

Theresa Watson also was aware that the President of the European Union, the Chancellor of Germany, would never again allow Britain to become part of the E.U. He had been against it from the start. It was only when the President of France urged him to let Britain be part that he had agreed.

But the head of MI6, Theresa Watson, was convinced that reentry into the E.U. was the only way her beloved country would survive. She would use all her resources to make it happen. That is why she had sent her man to Capri.

SOCHI, RUSSIA

The President of the Russian Federation lied on the beach of his favorite resort. His predecessors had built it, he had made the Olympics a great success, let the world know Russia was once more a world power. Clad in only a Speedo bathing suit he walked into the Black Sea. He loved the water, it gave him energy, it relaxed him. It was here, in the water, where he always designed his next move. Brexit was a gift from heaven, it had not been his idea, it should have been. That did not matter now. What mattered was how Russia could use it to its advantage. That was obvious, he knew. The E.U. represented a true threat to his mother Russia and he needed to do all to fragment the E.U. When he first learned that the Brits were contemplating leaving the E.U., he sent hundreds of his FBS agents, Russia's intelligence agency, the former KGB, into England. Their mission was simple: bribe everyone at Whitehall, even at Buckingham Palace, he now recalled with a smile. Bribe them all to lobby for Brexit. President Pavlov had spent billions of Rubles to have Britain leave the E.U. and he decided to spend more to have other countries do the same. Simple, he thought, a weak E.U. means a strong mother Russia.

CHAPTER IV

BERLIN, THE REICHSTAG

Prince Wilhelm of Hohenzollern, the chancellor of Germany and the President of the European Union sat at his favorite table at the Kaefer restaurant, the restaurant on the terrace of the Reichstag, Germany's parliament house. He came here each Thursday and always ordered his favorite meal, veal kloese. He enjoyed the dish with one of his favorite wines, a glass of "Gruener Veltiner". He loved the view overlooking some of Berlin, the home of his ancestors. Today, as he gazed at the city, he noticed all the cranes restoring buildings destroyed by the allies during World War II. The buildings his forefathers had built. Thank God the allies had decided to destroy all the buildings. The Prince knew the allies had seriously considered another plan, a plan designed to maintain the beautiful architecture of his forefathers, and instead destroy the people of Berlin. The plan had been to drop anthrax into the city killing all of its inhabitants. Buildings can be restored, he knew, lives could not.

The news that Britain had narrowly voted to leave the European Union was what Prince Wilhelm had prayed for. At the outset he had never wanted Britain to be part of it, but his friend and ally, the President of France, had pleaded with him to make Britain part of it. Then and now the Prince knew it was a mistake, a mistake that now was rectified, not by him but by the people of Britain. All during Britain's tenure in the EU had the former world power been a thorn in everyone's side, always asking for special considerations, not even accepting the Euro.

He snickered as he thought about the promises the new Premier, Margaret Sawyer, made to her people. Britain would demand special treatment from the E.U., favorite trade agreements, extraordinary deals on the immigrant issues. Good luck, the Prince thought as he took a small drink of his favorite wine.

He never understood the Royal family, a family like his of German heritage. From 1837 until 1917 the royal family was the House of Saxe-Coburg and Gothe, a German dynasty and a branch of the House of Wetlin, consisting of territories in present day Bavaria and Thuringia, Germany. But in 1917 George V changed the name to the House of Windsor, its current name. He did it in response to anti-German sympathies during WWI and to be more English sounding. For years the Royal family had sent their siblings to be educated in Germany and had married German princesses and often German was spoken within the walls of Buckingham Palace. Queen Victoria and Prince Albert only spoke German among each other. Although the Royal family is German, they did all to hide it. According to Norman Davis in "Vanished Kingdoms", the Royals honed their upper-class English accents, avoided German relatives and massaged the family tree beyond recognition.

Why would anyone want to ignore their heritage, their roots, the Prince never understood. Why had they fought each other so intensely? I guess, he thought, only family feuds would have that passion. Clearly massaging the family tree was not enough, killing the roots was more effective, more lasting. But now he held the upper hand. Today wars would not be won with armies, today the major weapon was the economy, and his country was the strongest in Europe. Yes, he knew, never would he allow Great Britain to become a member of the E.U. again. He would bring them to their knees, destroying their economy.

The Prince was late, he had spent too much time at the Kaefer. Today he was to address the Bundestag, his parliament, on the topic of Brexit. The restaurant was only steps away from where he was about to take the stage. Being a few minutes late was a privilege he enjoyed as the leader of Germany and the European Union.

CHAPTER V

WASHINGTON, D.C. THE WHITE HOUSE

"Brexit, Brexit tell me what does it mean?" the President of the United States asked as she leaned back in her chair behind the large desk in the Oval Office. Her Chief of Staff sat opposite her in the most powerful office of the world. He was in disbelief, no, not really. Never did he understand why the American people had elected Monica Drew. Clearly it was because of her husband, a former President. Her campaign had been difficult, most Americans believed that she was not honest, not trustworthy. Yet her campaign had been able to deflect all the scandals, her email disaster, her Foundation's questionable dealings, her poor record as Secretary of State. But it was her husband and money that allowed her to now sit in the Oval Office. No one had ever raised more money in a Presidential campaign than she did. And in America money buys all.

"Brexit means the exit of Great Britain from the EU," her Chief of Staff responded impatiently.

"The exit of Britain from the E.U.?" the President responded quizzically. "I did not know Britain was part of the E.U., are you sure? I know the Brit's currency is still the pound, not the Euro."

"Madame President," her Chief of Staff responded, "yes, Britain is part of the E.U. but chose not to change the currency."

"Well, anyhow, what does Brexit mean to us, how will it affect our country?"

"OK, first of all Britain's exit will take some time, the formal notification is a two-year process. Although the new Prime Minister of Britain has assured her country that she would initiate the exit as soon as possible. It is now clear that Britain is not ready to negotiate the terms of the exit. Current estimates indicate that it will not begin until the end of the year."

"Why does it take so long?" Monica Drew inquired.

"The process is complex. First, there are legal issues and free trade agreements with the E.U. have to be created as well as with 163 other nations of the World Trade Organization. Quotas, subsidies, tariffs, to mention but a few, need to be renegotiated. Britain at this time does not have the manpower, the trade negotiators, to do the job. So, Britain has to wait until it has all the players in place to invoke Article 50 of the E.U. treaty."

"What is Article 50?"

"Article 50 states that any member state may withdraw from the Union in accordance with its own constitutional requirements. A member State must notify the European Council of its intention and the Union shall then negotiate to conclude an agreement with that State. The agreement needs a qualified majority of the member states and the consent of the European parliament. No state has ever invoked article 50, yet. The timing of the withdrawal has become the major issue of contention, not only in the E.U., but in Britain as well. The E.U. clearly wants to see a quick withdrawal to prevent chaos, prevent other nations from leaving the E.U. But, as I said, Britain is not ready."

"Well, it all sounds very complex. Let's get down to what really matters, how does Brexit affect us, our country?" Monica Drew, now bored with her Chief of Staff's explanation, asked.

"According to our Federal Reserve chair, Brexit could have significant economic repercussions. Most economists agree that the impact would have a negative effect on our economy."

"That's incredible," the President exclaimed, "we, the U.S of America, the strongest nation in the world, cannot tell the Brits what to do?"

"No, Madame President, we cannot."

CHAPTER VI

CAPRI, ITALY

They were late, 15 minutes late. Adam did not want to leave, he wanted to stay in her arms and continue to make love. But Nicole reminded him of their dinner date and reluctantly Adam let go of her. Both entered the shower together in their luxurious apartment on the Island of Capri. Both decided to make love again as the hot water sprayed their naked bodies.

Nicole was beautiful, long black hair, blue eyes and the body of a model. She dressed in a tight, white dress she had bought not long ago on a trip to Milan. Adam too dressed in the cloth he had bought on the same trip, white Armani linen pants and a white linen shirt. Adam loved linen, loved the way it caressed his muscular body. Adam stood tall, 6 foot 2 inches, and he had the looks of a movie star.

The restaurant Adam had chosen was one of his favorites and only a short walk from his apartment perched high on a hill away from the heavy tourist area. Here he knew the menu, for Nicole and he ate there often. When they arrived the man from Britain was already sitting at the table Adam had reserved. His table, his Stammtisch, as he liked to call it, was located on the veranda overlooking the Tyrrhenian sea. The staff at the restaurant knew Nicole and Adam well, almost like friends, because Adam always made it a point to converse with them, inquire about their families, and he spoke Italian fluently.

The man from Britain got out of his chair and shook the hands of Nicole and Adam. No kiss on the cheek, Adam noticed, not the British way. The Brit was still dressed in a suit, not the same suit he had worn earlier, but a dark gray suit, a blue shirt and a red tie. Adam took his favorite seat, his back against the stone wall. Old habits never die, he thought. Always protect your back.

When the waiter approached Adam rose from his chair and embraced him, asking about the man's family, speaking in fluent Italian.

"Carlo, good to see you again, please meet my guest, a man for Britain."

The Brit rose from his chair almost embarrassed for he did not know whether to shake hands or embrace. He chose the former.

Nicole knew different, she hugged the waiter and kissed him on both cheeks.

"Let's have a cocktail before dinner." Adam suggested.

"The same as usual?" Carlo asked

"Yes, please for me and Nicole. And you Niguel?", the name the Brit had introduced himself with earlier in the day, "want the same?"

"Yes, please," he responded.

When the waiter left everyone took their seats. It was a beautiful evening, the sky filled with stars, a small breeze refreshing all.

"Thank you for joining me for dinner," the man from Britain, Niguel began. "I do not want to waste your time. Clearly you know our meeting earlier was not by chance. My government, Britain, has sent me here, so may I get to the point?"

"Of course," Adam responded. Nicole and he knew when the man had first approached them at the terrace of the Quisisana Hotel, that it was not a chance meeting. They did not discuss it because both knew, after all they had been trained by the best.

"I am with MI6 and I have been sent to recruit you."

"Well," Adam said, "you must know that we have retired, are no longer in the business."

"Yes," the man from MI6 responded, "but please hear me out."

The waiter, Carlo, approached and served the Campari all had ordered.

"Cheers," Niguel, the MI6 man, said as he raised his glass.

"Cheers," Nicole and Adam responded.

"I'll be short and right to the point," Britain's secret service man continued, "in my government, not all, but some, have decided that Brexit is a huge mistake. Leaving the E.U. will destroy our economy, our country. It is a mistake and we are determined to correct it. The vote to leave the E.U was an emotional one by the citizens of my country. It was an appeal made by the Royal family to bring Britain back to its former glory. Playing second fiddle to France and Germany in the E.U. was no longer acceptable to them."

"I thought one of the main reasons for Brexit was the migrant issue." Nicole interjected.

"No", Niguel answered. "The migrant issue was the excuse. And now the wall being built in Calais to keep the migrants out is a symbolic move to deceive that the migrant issue caused Brexit. The bottom line is Britain's survival depends on its return to the European Union."

"I realize that the vote was close, why not have another referendum?" Nicole inquired.

"That is the problem, why I am here," Niguel continued, "even if the British people voted overwhelmingly to reenter the E.U. it will not happen."

"Why," Nicole and Adam asked almost in unison.

"The President of the E.U., the Chancellor of Germany, is dead set against it. He never had wanted Britain to be part of it from the outset. It was the President of France, his friend, who had convinced him otherwise. But now, even he will block Britain. But the true obstacle is the German Chancellor."

"Why?" Adam asked, "what are his reasons?"

"I really don't know, I can only speculate," the MI6 man replied.

"It is true Britain was always a difficult member, always requesting privileged treatment, like not accepting the Euro as its currency. But we at MI6 believe the real reason lies in the past, in the feud within the royal families. Prince Wilhelm could never understand why the Royal family of Britain attempted to hide its German roots, deny them true heritage. I think he almost considers it treason."

"That seems irrational." Nicole interrupted, "history is history, it is the past."

"There is one thing I have learned," Niguel continued, "when it comes to relationships and royal families, little is ever forgiven and nothing is ever forgotten. Nonetheless, as long as Prince Wilhelm is in power Britain will never be part of the E.U. again."

"So, why did you come here, seek me out, how can I make a difference?" Adam asked.

By now Carlo, the waiter had approached to take their dinner orders. None had looked at the menu, all had been too engrossed in the conversation.

"I have a recommendation," Adam said as he handed his menu to the waiter. "Here they serve the best fish, better than anywhere. Why not let me order."

"You convinced me," Niguel said, "when in Rome do like the Romans do."

"Make that three," Nicole added.

"Carlo, to begin with we will have the potato cream soup with the seared lobster, for antipasti the Insalata Caprese, and for our primi and secondi piatti please serve us the risotto with Capri lemons and the fresh catch of the day, respectively. Of course, do not forget the wine, my favorite Pinot Grigio."

Carlo smiled, he had just won another bet, five Euros he and chef Antonio had waged on the meal Adam would order. Now he would win another five for he had already placed Adam's favorite Pinot Grigio in a bucket of ice.

"To summarize," Adam took up the conversation, "as long as Prince Wilhelm is around Britain has no chance of getting back in the E.U. If they don't, they are in real trouble, correct?"

"Yes", Niguel answered, "Britain will starve."

"So, what is the answer?" Adam asked, fully knowing what would come next.

"Simple, well not quite simple," the MI6 man replied, "that is why I am here. The President of the E.U., Prince Wilhelm has to be eliminated."

"Eliminated, what do you mean?" Adam asked, fully aware of the meaning of elimination. He had heard it before, it had been his business.

"To be direct, he needs to be assassinated!" Niguel said almost in a whisper.

"Assassinate Prince Wilhelm?" Adam whispered, feigning complete surprise. "What will happen next?"

"Well", the man from MI6 replied. "It is clear that the Prince will be succeeded by another noble, Herzog or Duke von Claussen, who is married to a granddaughter of the Queen, Princess Sarah. The Duke is very close to the royal family and will do all to help Britain."

"OK, so you came here to ask me to assassinate the President of the E.U., the German Chancellor, Prince Wilhelm?"

Now Nicole interjected with a smile, "why don't you send James Bond, your 007?"

"007 is currently deep into something," Niguel responded laughing.

"But, seriously, the job will be very difficult. Only the best has a chance at success, a small chance. That is why we want Adam, we at MI6 are convinced there is not one better. Furthermore, the kill should take place in Berlin, a place Adam knows like the back of his hand. And to convince you even further we are willing to pay 60 million pounds, 30 million when you agree and 30 million when the job is done."

'Well, the price is enticing, but I don't kill just for money. I only kill for the challenge," Adam explained, "and this certainly is a challenge like few others."

Now Carlo approached to serve Adam's favorite meal. No one spoke as they silently enjoyed their food.

"A wonderful meal and a wonderful evening," Nicole rekindled the conversation, but also wanted to change the topic.

"Well, I like to see you guys bet each other on who will win the UEFA champions league."

"Before I tell you my pick I would like to know whether Adam will accept the assignment," Niguel replied.

"Right now I do not know, I need a little time to think about it, to discuss it with Nicole," Adam said as he gestured for Carlo, the waiter. "A limoncello, anyone?" Adam asked. All agreed to end the beautiful evening with a glass of limoncello.

"Fair enough," the man from Britain responded to Adam's request for a little time, "but there is not much time," the MI6 man emphasized, "we believe that the start of the Berlin marathon on the last weekend of September, may be our best opportunity. The race will begin at the Brandenburg Gate. The chancellor is scheduled to start the race. No doubt large crowds will line the starting area, as well as about 40-50,000 participants. Also, our agents have researched the area and determined that the Hotel Adlon on the Pariser Platz, next to the Brandenburg Gate, would be the perfect spot from where to take the shot. Nothing obstructs the view and the Brandenburg Gate is about 100 meters away. MI6 has already rented a room there overlooking the Platz. I am told it is the perfect vantage point. But I am not telling anything you don't already know, you know Berlin like the back of your hand."

"What a coincidence," Adam mused. "Nicole and I have plans to be in Berlin then to enjoy Puccini's 'Tosca' at the Staatsoper in the Schiller Theater that very weekend. We are staying at my favorite hotel, the Regent, on the Gendarmenmarkt."

Was it merely coincidence or was it fate, Adam wondered.

"OK, "Adam said as all rose to leave the restaurant, "let me sleep on it."

He leaned over, picked up his glass of Lemoncello and finished it.

CHAPTER VII

LONDON, ENGLAND, 85 ALBERT EMBANKMENT, VAUXHALL

Her phone rang, she glanced at the clock on her desk in her office of SIS, Special Intelligence Services of Great Britain or MI6. It was 9 P.M., but Theresa Watson never left her office before 10 P.M. She was a workaholic and she knew that this phone call was important. She was right, the call came from Capri, Italy. Her agent was brief.

"All worked according to plan, he is considering it. He loves money, but more, he loves challenges. We will know very soon." A click, the call was over.

CAPRI, ITALY

When Nicole and Adam returned to their apartment, all Adam wanted was to make love to her. He needed to clear his mind, forget all, relax, and there was no better way to do it than to have sex with Nicole. They had barely entered their apartment when he began to kiss her, not on the mouth, but he kissed her on her neck, gently stroking her face. But Nicole was more anxious, she could not wait for him to enter her. She stripped off his clothes, Adam naked now, his penis erect, was aroused. He lifted her and carried Nicole into the bedroom. He did not undress her, but he simply raised her skirt, lied on top of her and entered her. Their love making was short, both had lost control, both had orgasms after only several minutes.

Adam rolled over, clearly his mind was preoccupied, Nicole thought. Never had their love making been so quick, so short. Adam always loved extensive foreplay, foreplay that always resulted in Nicole experiencing several orgasms.

"Nicole," he said, "I am sorry, but I have a lot on my mind."

"I understand," she responded. "But don't apologize, I enjoyed every moment."

"Let's have a Grappa on the terrace. It is a beautiful night. Let's appreciate the sea, the waves as they gently roll towards shore. They always remind me of peace, how gentle nature can be."

"Yes," Nicole responded, "it is your decision, peace or war."

Both had put on a bathrobe and Adam walked to the bar to fill two glasses with his favorite Grappa. He walked onto the terrace which overlooked the beautiful sea, the bay of Napoli. He kissed Nicole on the mouth and then handed her the glass of Grappa.

"Nicole, I need your help. This assignment, I am not sure of what to do. It is a lot of money, but we are comfortable now, we don't need the money. But it is the challenge that really interests me. It is like taking the last penalty kick in the World Cup soccer game to win it all. I don't think I can resist it."

"Adam, the decision is all yours."

"What troubles me is that the target is Prince Wilhelm, a man who once hired me to protect him, a man I really like, yet I want to take the assignment, it is the greatest challenge I have ever faced. I think I need to do it, to prove to myself that I am truly the best. That matters more to me than anything else. Nicole, I want to do it."

"I always knew you did," Nicole said as she leaned over and kissed Adam.

CHAPTER VIII

BERLIN, GERMANY

Nicole and Adam sat on the terrace of one of the many cafés lining the banks of the river Spree in the Nikolai district of Berlin. Both we're enjoying one of their favorite aperitifs, Campari and orange juice. Both were dressed elegantly. Nicole wore a tight, strapless dress which accentuated her beautiful body, her long black hair she wore in a ponytail. Adam wore his favorite dark blue Armani suit, a white shirt and a blue pin striped tie. Tonight, they were going to enjoy Puccini's opera, Tosca, at the Schiller Theater, an event they had planned to attend months ago. Adam and Nicole loved opera and each year they attended one in Berlin, always at the beginning of the opera season, late September.

It had been a busy day for Adam. When he returned to the Regent Hotel after his failed assassination of Prince Wilhelm and his evasive boat trip on the river Spree, Nicole greeted him anxiously. Niguel, she had informed him, had called and had asked her to go to a public phone on the corner of Friedrichstrasse and Charlottenstrasse, only a very short walk from the Regent Hotel. As soon as she reached the phone booth the phone rang. It was Niguel, his message was brief.

Have Adam go to the Spreewald tomorrow, have him be there at 10 A.M. A man will be waiting, it is important, was the message.

Adam had immediately contacted one of the concierge's of the hotel and ordered a car, a large car, a Mercedes 600. Adam loved to drive and he loved the large Mercedes.

SPREEWALD, GERMANY

The Spreewald is located only 100km south-east of Berlin. It was designated a biosphere reserve by Unesco in 1991. It is known for its traditional irrigation system consisting of more than 200 small canals more than 1300 km long. Its landscape was formed during the ice age. It is an area of forests and wetlands and pine forests on sandy dry areas. About 50,000 people live there, most descendants of Slavic tribes, who have preserved their traditional language and customs and clothing. The main industry today is tourism and small boats with guides travers the canals daily.

Adam had been there often but most he remembered when he was in grammar school at the Lanz-Schule in Dahlem, his teacher had instructed each student to create a replica of a Spreewaldhaus. His grandmother then took him to see the Spreewald to study the houses. Many had thatched roofs and wooden exteriors. Adam had made sketches trying to build the replica.

The man was already there. Adam had arrived early, 15 minutes early. The Brit was already sitting in the boat, a small wooden boat. It reminded Adam of the gozzo boat Adam always rented on Capri, but there was no lounge area in the bow of the boat and it had no motor.

As soon as Adam stepped on board, the ferryman pushed his boat into the Spree River.

"We can speak here freely in English; our ferryman won't understand a single word. I made sure," the man from Britain said.

"And I will be brief," the high-ranking member of Britain's parliament, a man who often was asked to 10 Downing Street for consultation, began.

"Unfortunately, our new Prime Minister is myopic, does not see the implications of Brexit. She is only focused on Britain. Clearly, Brexit was financed by the Russians. They paid all the politicians. Russia wants to keep Britain out of the European Union. But that is only the first step in Mr. Pavlov's plan. The purpose is to disassemble the E.U. A weak E.U. is better than no E.U. and it will make Russia once more the most dominant force in Europe."

The ferryman now steered the boat along the narrow river anxious to show his occupants all the sights. Adam was silent, anxious to hear what the Brit had to say.

"Since Russia does not want the Brits back in the E.U.," the man continued, "Prince Wilhelm, the staunch advocate to keep Britain out, has become an asset to Mr. Pavlov. Yet my boss, the head of MI6, is convinced that if Britain is to survive, once again it needs to be a full member of the E.U."

Adam now was a bit puzzled, had this man, this high-ranking minister of Britain's parliament, not been sent here by MI6?

The Brit read his mind.

"You wonder why I am here, why I am telling you all this. But it is quite simple. Since you failed to assassinate Prince Wilhelm, and even if you were successful, MI6 had to erase all traces leading back to them. You have to be eliminated. Surely you must have thought of it. I am here to tell you that your assassination is to take place tonight while you are attending Tosca, Puccini's opera."

"Why are you telling me this?"

"Well," the minister replied, "I really don't work for MI6, they think I do. But I work for the Russians. Always have since they first recruited me while I was at Oxford. It is not that I believe in their ideology, I am a realist and a capitalist. I believe in money and Russia pays very well."

Adam was surprised, how can you betray your country for money, he thought, but then he realized he had done the same, not always just for money, but also for the challenge.

"Please," the British minister instructed the ferryman in fluent German, "let's return."

"Return?" the man at the stern of the boat, the ferryman, clad in the traditional clothing of the Spreewald, asked in disbelief.

"I have not yet shown you the beautiful Spreewald."

"We have seen all that fancies us." The minister, the man paid by the FSB, Russia's intelligence agency, replied as he handed the guide a one hundred Euro note.

BERLIN, GERMANY

There was much commotion, police boats on the River Spree, sirens, police rushing the river bank. Adam carried his opera glasses, the ones he had brought to watch Puccini's Tosca. He focused on the man the police had just retrieved from the river. He was shocked, no doubt, it was the man he had just met hours ago in the Spreewald, the minister from Britain. Adam was now on full alert, Puccini had to wait for another time. He and Nicole had to leave at once. Clearly MI6's time table had changed.

"Nicole, we need to leave now." He whispered in her ear. Nicole knew what now meant.

Adam did not wait for the bill but left a 50 Euro note on the table, more than the bill had called for. Both quickly walked toward Friedrichstrasse and Adam hailed a cab.

"The Hauptbahnhof," Adam instructed the driver, "quickly, please, we are in a hurry, don't want to miss our train."

The driver smiled as he took the 50 Euro note for a 10 Euro ride.

Adam kept staring out of the rear window of the Mercedes cab as it sped towards Berlin's main train station. No one followed, no one he could detect. But he knew the best would never be seen and surely the best was following him.

Adam had decided the train station was the best option. It was a weekend, Berlin's marathon, and surely the station would be busy with travelers. He was right. Tourists were arriving and leaving Berlin, the station was almost chaotic.

Adam asked Nicole to go to one of the counters and purchase two first class tickets to Moscow. He went to a different counter and purchased two first class sleeping car tickets to Naples. He had studied the train schedule, both were to leave at the same time. It was a diversion, one he knew had little chance to succeed. Both had no luggage, all had been left behind at the Regent Hotel. Nicole entered the train to Moscow, walked through the restaurant car and left the train only minutes before its departure. She rapidly took the stairway to the next platform, to where the train to Naples via Munich was about to leave. She was the last passenger to enter the train. Or was she?

Adam and Nicole settled in their sleeping compartment as the train slowly left the station. Adam was convinced no one had followed them. Yet he had to make sure. He raised the window shade in his compartment to overlook the platform. That's when he saw him, a tall muscular man dressed in black jeans, a black T-shirt sprinting to reach the train. With his right hand the man grabbed the handle of the last car's door and jumped onto the train. Now Adam knew he had been followed, now he knew his trip to Naples would not be peaceful.

At 7:49 P.M. the train left Berlin's Hauptbahnhoff and Nicole and Adam were hungry. But more importantly Adam wanted to draw out his opponent, he wanted to face him. Adam and Nicole entered the dining car of the train at 8:15 P.M. The car was elegant, white table cloths covered the tables, the waiters were dressed in black tie. The car was almost empty and Adam chose a table at one end of the car. He took a seat with his back to the wall as was his habit. He asked Nicole to sit opposite him but near the aisle, to give her more mobility if she needed it.

As soon as they took their seats, a black tied waiter approached them. He was young, blond, six-foot-tall, blue eyes and an outgoing smile.

"A drink before dinner?" he asked in German.

"Yes, please," Adam replied.

"Sparkling water for both of us and the menu please."

"Danke schoen," the waiter replied.

As he walked away Adam noticed the man's gate, athletic, his body muscular not the build of your usual waiter he thought. But clearly, he was not the man he had seen jumping onto the train as it left the station. Nonetheless, Adam knew he had to be cautious. He had been trained by the best.

"What an unusual waiter," Nicole said with a smile, "do all German trains only employ athletes?"

"You noticed as well," Adam responded. "I think we are going to have a sleepless night."

The young waiter returned, served the sparkling water, and took their order. Wiener schnitzel for both with pommes frites and a glass of one of Adam's favorite white wines, a Pinot Grigio.

"A great choice," the young waiter responded, "my favorite wine as well."

Dinner was served quickly. The train's staff was aware that the passengers wanted to catch some sleep on their 12-hour trip.

"Here is the Schnitzel, one of our best meals, you made the right choice." The young, muscular waiter said, as he placed the plates in front of his passengers.

"And here is the wine, my favorite," he smiled.

Adam took his glass and poured a small amount into the water glass he had not used.

"Please," he said, "have a drink. Tell me if it is as good as you promised."

"No," the waiter responded. "I am not allowed while on duty."

"I insist," Adam said. "I won't tell anyone."

"Sir," the waiter now clearly uncomfortable, "I could get fired."

"All right, I guess we just take you word that this is a special wine. Thank you."

The waiter left, almost in a hurry, Adam thought.

"Nicole, don't drink the wine. I think it is over the hill."

"I agree," Nicole said with a smile, "the bouquet is different."

Both enjoyed their schnitzel and the pommes frites. When they finished their meal, another waiter approached and cleared the table.

"You did not enjoy your wine?" he asked as he glanced at both of the full glasses.

"No ", Adam replied. "We changed our minds. Wine keeps us awake and we want to enjoy a good night's sleep. But thank you and good night."

The waiter, an older man, frail, short stature, and with a black mustache smiled, "Well, have a good night," he said as he accepted the 20 Euro note Adam handed him.

Adam was disappointed. He had been certain that the man who had jumped onto the train would enter the dining car. But he did not. When Nicole and he entered their sleeping compartment he told Nicole he would take a short walk, examine the cars. He wanted to be the hunter, not the hunted. Nicole wanted to go along, but Adam refused. Lock the door and only open it when you hear my voice, he advised her.

Adam left their compartment and walked towards the dining car. Again, he expected the man who had earlier jumped onto the train to be there. He was not. The dining car was busy now, almost all tables were occupied. Adam continued and entered the next car. There was a toilet to his right, the door barely open. That's when he saw the man, the small waiter with the mustache, lying on the floor, a broken wine glass next to him. Adam leaned down his right hand feeling for the pulse in the man's neck. There was none. I guess Nicole and I were right, he thought, the wine was over the hill. And now he was reassured. He had been followed and these men meant business. Already there had been one man floating in the Spree river, another drinking the wrong wine.

As Adam was about to return to his compartment he saw two men on the platform separating the dining car and Adam's sleeping car. It was the young, muscular waiter and the fellow who had jumped onto the train as it had left the Hauptbahnh of. Both appeared to be involved in an argument. Both were shouting at each other, both had their back to Adam. Adam reached for his gun which he carried holstered above his left ankle, his favorite Beretta, the gun of the Mossad. He opened the door to the platform of the train and both of his adversaries turned at once reaching for their weapons. But Adam did not hesitate. One shot into the forehead of each man, four more shots into each body. The Mossad way, Israel's famed intelligence agency, which had trained him. Adam used his feet to kick both bodies off the speeding train. Now, he thought, maybe I can get some sleep, as he walked back to his compartment to join Nicole.

CHAPTER IX

NAPLES, ITALY

The train from Berlin to Naples arrived on time. 7:30 a.m. Neither Adam nor Nicole had slept much. Both had decided to alternate watch, four hours on, and four hours off. Both knew the game. Yes, they had eliminated the immediate threat, but both knew there would be more.

It was much like cancer Adam told Nicole as they took the early ferry boat to Capri, their home. Just like cancer, you can kill a few cells but to kill cancer you have to kill the source. And it was the source Nicole and Adam had to eliminate. And just like cancer it would be a difficult task. Yet to be cured, to be no longer hunted, they had little choice. They had to kill the source who wanted them dead. They had to assassinate Theresa Watson, the head of MI6.

CAPRI, ITALY

He slept like a baby. The best sleep he had had in weeks. Here he felt safe, not only because he lived on a small island, not because each electronic device plausible protected his apartment, it was the sea, the sea below that gave him peace. The blue sea, the calm water, the vastness, the gentle waves always calmed his mind, relaxed his body, released all of his tensions, made him feel rejuvenated, made him feel almost born again. Nicole and Adam slept all day until the sun set on the bay of Naples. As Adam stepped out of the shower he again realized the veracity of what the British Minister had told him in the Spreewald. At first Adam had doubted the man, but when he witnessed the dead man's body being fished out of the river Spree in Stadt Mitte of Berlin, he knew the man had spoken the truth.

MI6 had hired him to assassinate Prince Welhellm to facilitate Britain's reentry into the European Union. And he had failed. Now MI6 had no choice. It was imperative to erase all traces that could lead back to them. If it became public knowledge that Britain's Secret Intelligence Service had attempted to kill Prince Wilhelm, the head of E.U., their attempt to reenter the European Union would fail for good. No, Adam reflected, MI6 had no choice, they had to kill him, and Adam also knew that they would succeed. Even he could not escape an intelligence agency with vast resources. Adam took a large, white Polo bath towel engraved with the letter "H" out of one of the cabinets in his large bathroom. He had bought a dozen of them when he and Nicole last stayed in Rome at the Hassler Hotel. He had liked the softness of the towel, the way it felt when he dried his body. Hassler's concierge had obliged when Adam asked to purchase a few towels.

Adam did not dry himself thoroughly, he was anxious. He wanted to sit down on his balcony overlooking the sea and discuss their predicament with Nicole. Adam was anxious for he had no answer, perhaps Nicole did. He had learned that women often saw problems from a different angle, often solving complex ones with ease.

He put on a white bathrobe which he had also bought at the Hassler Hotel, walked into his kitchen and prepared coffee. It was the aroma of the coffee which awoke Nicole. He asked Nicole not to shower, not yet, for he was anxious to speak with her.

Nicole joined Adam, she was also clad only in one of Hassler's bathrobes, her long black hair falling gently on her shoulders. Adam leaned over and kissed her lightly on the mouth.

"Nicole," Adam began the conversation, "Nicole, we are in a terrible predicament. I am convinced that MI6 intends to eliminate both of us. They have no choice and I have no answer."

"I agree," Nicole responded without hesitation, but unlike you I do have an answer."

"You do?" Adam asked in disbelief.

"Yes, it really is quite simple. But I am starving. Why don't you prepare tortilla espanola for us, choose a bottle of red wine, and then we shall talk."

Nicole loved to tease Adam and made him wait to hear her answer.

"Please, Nicole, not now. I need to know."

"OK, but I will only give you an appetizer and explain it all after you feed me," she said with a smile.

"It's a deal," he responded anxiously. He could not wait to hear what Nicole had to say.

"It really is very simple," Nicole continued, enjoying every moment of it.

"Simple?"

"You must go to the man you tried to kill, Prince Wilhelm. He knows you well, respects you. I am sure he will receive you."

"See the man I tried to assassinate? Are you serious or playing a game?"

"Quite serious," she responded.

"OK, I'll go and see the Prince, then what?"

"That I will tell you after we eat. Now it is up to you to honor our deal. Go and prepare the food please," she said as she leaned over and kissed him on the mouth.

"Nicole, please, tell me now."

"A deal is a deal. Your next move is the kitchen, and please hurry, if I starve to death you will never know the answer. While you prepare the food, I will take a shower."

Adam had no choice. He knew Nicole could be stubborn. He got up to walk into the kitchen to fetch the wine and prepare their favorite meal.

Nicole and Adam sat on the terrace overlooking the beautiful Mediterranean Sea. It was a full moon, a moon that illuminated the sea. Both enjoyed Adam's meal, both had been hungry. As Adam took another sip of his favorite red wine, a Chianti Classico, he was anxious to understand Nicole's solution.

"Go to Prince Wilhelm and tell him I was the assassin who tried to kill him, am I correct, is that your solution?" Adam asked not in disbelief, but now seeing the merit of it.

"Exactly," Nicole responded, "that is how we will disarm MI6, now they can no longer kill you and I. If they do, it will only give credibility to a story they surely want to deny."

"Brilliant", Adam responded, "what would I ever do without you? But what do you think the Prince's reaction will be?"

"I have no idea, but let's find out!"

CHAPTER X

CAPRI, ITALY

Adam knew MI6 was nearby. But he also knew he could outsmart them, after all he had been trained by the best, the NSA and the Mossad. Leaving Capri on a tourist boat to go to Naples was not a choice. Surely MI6 agents were already in place. Adam designed a different plan. He asked his friend, Victorino, the captain of his favorite gozzo, a small fishing boat, to meet him at the Marina Piccola. The marina was only a few hundred yards from Adam's apartment. Steep steps leading to it. Adam had also asked Victorino to have his cousin, Alberto, meet them at the Blue Grotto. Alberto owned a speed boat, a boat that would carry Adam and Nicole to Naples.

All went according to plan. When the MI6 man who was stationed only steps from Adam's apartment followed them to Marina Piccola, he was certain Nicole and Adam were about to take a day trip around the island of Capri, an excursion done by many of the tourists. Yet he took no chance, he also ordered a gozzo to follow Nicole and Adam. Unfortunately for him the gozzo he ordered was owned by Victorino's cousin. The instructions had been direct, being 30 minutes late to pick up the MI6 man, the 30 minutes Nicole and Adam needed to get to the speed boat to Naples.

Adam also realized that MI6 men would be stationed at the port of Naples, expecting him and Nicole to disembark from the ferry ship carrying passengers back to Naples from Capri. The speed boat did not make its landing at the main dock in the harbor of Naples, but instead docked at one of the many small docks occupied by small fishing boats. And Adam did not order a cab, instead he and Nicole used a small Vespa scooter Victorino's cousin had parked only a few meters from where the boat made shore. The scooter, Adam knew would not be his ultimate transportation to Berlin. Nicole had laughed at the thought. But taking the train, or an airplane from Naples would be dangerous, surely MI6 had covered all those means of escape. So, a long scooter ride was their best way of escape. Well, not that long a ride. Victorino had family in the town of Villagio only 50 miles from Naples. There Adam would be given a powerful motorcycle, a BMW 1500. Adam's plan was to ride to Rome and then take the train to Berlin.

Adam rode the scooter at full speed to the dismay of Nicole sitting behind him and holding on for dear life. They rode through the beautiful landscape, along the shore of the Mediterranean. But, neither noticed. Both were focused on their escape. In Villagio, at the restaurant Arosa, the bike was waiting for him, just as Victorino had promised. There was no one attending the bike but the key was in the ignition. It was a BMW F800GT, black metallic, a true racing machine with a speed of 125 mph plus. The trip to Rome was no less than 110 miles away. In an hour Adam thought, at full throttle, he could be at Rome's train station to take the next train to Berlin. But there was no rush, Adam thought. He had skillfully evaded all of MI6's men. A leisure ride on one of his favorite machines, the BMW motorcycle, he intended to enjoy.

But Adam was wrong. While in Capri the MI6 man had attached a small chip to Nicole's purse, a purse she always wore, a purse that she now shouldered as she rode with Adam on the powerful BMW motorcycle, on their way to escape.

When Adam reached Fiumicino, Rome's airport, he left the bike at the entrance of the main terminal, as Victorino had instructed him to do. And immediately he saw the two men, all dressed in black, muscular, clearly MI6 agents. Adam was puzzled, there was no way they could have followed him. He had taken all the precautions, all the tricks he had learned while at the NSA and the Mossad. Now he knew it was a chip, someone had planted it on him or Nicole. There was no other explanation.

"Nicole," he requested, "go to the bathroom, strip, find the chip MI6 planted on you or I. I will do the same." Nicole did not have to undress as she emptied her favorite purse, one she always carried, she saw the chip. No, she did not see it, but she felt it. A chip, small in size, had been placed where the strap attached to her Gucci bag.

"Adam, "she said, "they had a chip in my purse, sorry."

"Not your fault," he replied. "But now we need to find a new way to lose them. Keep the chip, it will help us."

Clearly MI6 had anticipated that Adam would meet Prince Wilhelm at the Reichstag, Germany's parliament in Berlin. This is where Adam would lead them. He asked Nicole, her chip still in her favorite purse, to go to the Kaefer, the restaurant on the terrace of Berlin's parliament house.

As predicted, MI6 was there, a man and a woman having lunch on the terrace, two more men occupying a table inside the restaurant and three more men strolling outside the entrance to the Kaefer, strolling on the spacious open terrace which surrounded the magnificent building.

85 ALBERT EMBANKMENT VAUXHALL, LAMBETH

Theresa Watson received the phone call at once, it was 12:10 p.m. London time. She knew the luncheon date in Berlin, where her agents would find Adam and the Prince, had been set for 1:00 p.m. Berlin time. An hour later than Big Ben would announce. The head of MI6 had planned meticulously, to have the three people she needed to eliminate in one place, was a stroke of good old English luck. Clearly, she had thought, the Gods fancy me. But she was wrong, it was the Irish who always enjoyed the luck, not the British.Theresa's plan had been simple. All needed to look like a terrorist attack, an attack by ISIS, the terrorist organization which had been responsible for many brutal attacks in Europe only months ago. MI6 knew all the leaders of the terrorist organization, contact was easy.

SOUTH BEIRUT, LEBANON

The Secretary General of Hezbollah, Hassan Nasral, sat in his underground bunker, a bunker he seldom left, afraid of the Israeli drones designed to kill him. Hezbollah, the party of God, had been created as an alternative to the Christian-Sunni government, which his people, the Shiites, loathed. But he also loathed the Americans, he loathed all of the nonbelievers, all who did not believe in his god, Allah.

Hassan had been elated when he learned that the British, MI6, wanted him to kill the President of the E.U., the chancellor of Germany. The British had informed him that the kill would take place at the Reichstag, in Berlin, in the heart of Germany. Do not just kill the man, but also destroy much of the building, he had been instructed. The President of the E.U. would be accompanied by two other people, a man and a woman. Both as well had to die.

Hassan had not believed his good fortune. The Brits assured easy access for his terrorist, no problem entering the E.U., Germany, Berlin. MI6 would take care of it. Hassan had first considered using his brother-in-law, Imad Mughdial, for the job. Imad was a brutal enforcer having masterminded the bombing of the U.S. embassy in Beirut in 1983, the hijacking of TWA flight 847 in 1985, the Khobar Towers building in Saudi Arabia, the kidnapping of many Israeli soldiers and more.

But Hassan knew that to kill the President of the European Union,and to destroy Germany's parliament building would be as devastating as the destruction of the twin towers in Manhattan, New York. For this mission he needed the best, one he could trust, one of his blood-line, one he loved. It would be the greatest sacrifice he could make to his god Allah. He chose his grandson, Ali, for the mission. Ali had lived in the U.S., was educated at Stanford and Ali would blend in as the perfect American tourist. And Ali would wear a heavy suicide vest, a vest that would kill all, a vest that would send his grandson to heaven, to enjoy all of the 70 virgins Allah promised.

TEL AVIV, ISRAEL

The head of the Mossad, Israels' famous intelligence agency, had learned about the plot to take place at the Reichstag in Berlin, Maza Sharef was not sure of what to make of it. He knew that there was much controversy regarding Brexit at Whitehall, Britain's parliament. But would they attempt to hire Hezbollah, kill the E.U. President? He doubted it. But to make sure he decided to contact his friend at the CIA, director William Peter Davis, "Pistol Pete", as he was affectionately called by his friends.

LANGLEY, VIRGINIA

Pistol Pete answered the phone at once. His counterpart, the head of the Mossad, did not call often.

"Tell me, what is this all about, the assassination of the President of the E.U. Is it for real?" Maza, head of the Mossad, asked.

"We don't know," Pistol Pete replied, "we think it is a hoax, a distraction. But we do believe Hezbollah intends to strike us."

"I agree," the head of the Mossad responded, "but keep me informed and I will do the same. "

A clique, no goodbyes.

SANSSOUCI, POTSDAM

Prince Wilhelm had asked to occupy a small room, Friedrich the Great's library, to meet with Adam. It was a private room not open to the public. It was a privilege only he enjoyed, the descendant of the "Alter Fritz" as king Friedrich the Second was remembered by his Berliners. Schloss Sanssouci had not been closed down for the meeting between Adam and the Prince. On the contrary, both wanted all to be as usual.

"Prince," Adam began the conversation "This is probably the most difficult day of my life."

"Please," Wilhelm responded, "relax, we are friends."

"You need to know, Prince, that I am a professional killer. Yes, I kill for money, but more importantly I kill for the challenge. The more important my kill, the more money I get, but also the challenge is greater and the risks."

"I understand," the Prince nodded as he asked for one of the attendants to serve them a glass of wine. "Why did you come here, why did you want to meet with me?"

"I will be direct,"Adam responded,"I will pull no punches. MI6 hired me to kill you. The flesh wound on your right cheek was my shot, I missed."

The Prince leaned back in his chair, a chair only Friedrich the Great had sat in, and calmly he continued the conversation.

"You missed?" he asked with a smile, "I have been told you are the best, never miss a shot."

"You are right. Fortunately for you I made a mistake."

"Well," the Prince interjected, "not just fortunately for me, but fortunately for the E.U. Please, hear me out. I want you to understand what the E.U. is all about. The E.U. is not about me or Germany. The E.U. is all about establishing a balance of power, not only in Europe, but in the world. But let's talk about Europe first. Clearly Russia wants to be a world power again, but to succeed Russia needs to disassemble Europe, Britain was their first target, an easy one. Mr. Pavlov, the President of the Russian Federation, is not only a smart politician, but he knows how to get things done. He does it the KGB way, now the FBS, where he was once the head. He knows that Britain feels like a substitute player, sitting on the bench, playing second fiddle to France and Germany. And he knows the British people, particularly their royalty, do not like it. All remember as Britain once was, a major power dominating much of the world. Yet times have changed. Wars are no longer fought with weapons, wars are won by economic strength. And Britain does not have it."

The prince now got out of his chair, paced the small room his forefathers had occupied. "Britain will never be able to join the E.U. again," the Prince said emphatically.

"But why?" Adam wanted to know.

"Britain's departure from the E.U. was not the wish of the British people, it was a plan designed by Mr. Pavlov, the President of the Russian Federation. He paid many rubles to British politicians to make it happen. Already his agents are bribing other governments, Greece, Spain and more, to leave the E.U. A weak E.U. means a strong Russia. And what astonishes me the most is that your government, the U.S. does not understand world politics. Maybe I should not be so surprised, look at what the U.S. has done in the Middle East."

Adam too now took a drink from the glass of wine sitting on the table that had not been used for more than 250 years.

"I think I now understand, for Russia it is important to have Britain leave the E.U. Just a first step to disassemble the E.U. But, why is Britain so anxious to do it? Why did Russia pick Britain to be the first?"

"Britain," the Prince responded, "was never a staunch supporter of the E.U. Britain always wanted special treatment, always thought because of her heritage, she needed to be treated with white gloves. As you know, I always resisted Britain becoming part of the E.U., it was only on the behest of my friend the President of France, that I agreed. But now he and I are in accord, no more Britain in the E.U., we need a unified European Union where all of us are on the same page."

Prince Wilhelm walked back and sat back in his chair, a chair no one has sat in for centuries.

"OK," Adam said, "where do we go from here?" Adam now was convinced that the Prince understood politics, not just European politics, but politics that would have an impact on the world.

"Adam, the Prince continued, "my mission is to make peace, peace not only in Europe, but peace in the world. And peace can only be accomplished by the balance of power. No one nation can be allowed to dominate, not even your country, the United States of America."

"I agree", Adam replied in awe of the Prince's view on geopolitics," where do I fit in. I would like to join your team. I think you have the answer for peace."

"Simple," the Prince replied with a smile, "you tried to kill me, but now I want you to protect my ass. I want you to be in charge of my security."

Both raised their wine glasses, both made peace in Friedrich the Great's library.

CHAPTER XI

BERLIN, GERMANY, THE KAEFER

Nicole had arrived early. She knew all the MI6 agents would be in place, her chip had led the way. The young Arab, dressed in a suit to hide his suicide vest, took a table only a few feet from Nicole. He too recognized all the MI6 agents, all placed in strategic locations at the restaurant. He was sweating, perspiration dropping from his face. It was not particularly warm on this Berlin September day but the weight of his armor made him sweat. As soon as you occupy the table next to the President of the E.U. and his two companions, pull the trigger, he has been instructed. Yet he hesitated. There was only Nicole, not the other two men he had been told would be there. Ali did not order lunch, just sparkling water he told the pretty young waitress as she approached his table.

Ali waited for 10 minutes as he drank from the glass of Pelligrino. No one else joined Nicole's table. Ali knew that their plot had gone arrey. He put a 10 Euro note on the table and left the restaurant, strolling slowly towards the elevator. There he joined the many tourists who had enjoyed their visit to the Bundestag building. Ali was anxious to get back to his hotel, the Askanischer Hof, on the Kudam of Berlin. Ali had chosen the hotel carefully. He had wanted to avoid the larger, more glamorous hotels in Berlin. Ali needed to stay under the radar and the small boutique hotel would help him to do so. When he checked into the hotel two weeks ago, he had used his American passport, a passport he had acquired because his mother was an American, born and raised in California. Ali had told the receptionist that he was in Berlin to enroll at the Humboldt Universitaet in the center of the city. Ali's English was perfect, the language he always spoke with his mother.

Ali did not take the taxi from the Reichstag but he took public transportation, Bus 100. The bus ride was short but Ali was covered with perspiration, the suicide vest was heavy loaded with explosives not to only kill Germany's chancellor but also designed to destroy much of the building. When he entered the large room of his boutique hotel he quickly discarded the lethal bomb. Ali had not worn the vest when he went to Kaefer. Here security was tight. In order to access the building, he had to submit a copy of his passport days ahead. His weapon of destruction had gained access to the Kaefer via air. The day before the start of the Berlin Marathon helicopters covered the sky over Stadt Mitte, advertising, celebrating the upcoming event. It was after hours, the Reichstag had just been closed to all tourists, the last just leaving the building. That's when the chopper hired by Hezbollah, dropped the package onto the terrace of the Reichstag building, barely, for the package almost missed the terrace of the building, one of the straps caught the guard rail on the expansive terrace holding the vest in place. A security guard, hired by Hezbollah, retrieved the bomb and placed it in the place the conspirators had agreed upon. The guard quickly took the vest and carried it to one of the public bathrooms. Here he earlier had emptied the toilet bowl of all water, and here he placed the bomb. Just to be certain Hezbollah had made sure the suicide bomb was covered in a water proof enclosure.

Then the guard covered the bowl with its lid, locked the door to the bathroom, placed a sign on the outside of the door, "Out of use, under repair", the sign proclaimed. The guard also placed a yellow tape, a do not enter tape, across the door. Ali had used the duplicate key he had been given to enter the toilet, had retrieved the vest and strapped it under his baggy jacket.

TEL AVIV, ISRAEL

"Pete, we have some new information," the head of the Mossad informed his counterpart of the CIA on their secure telephone line. "The Secretary General of Hezbollah sent his grandson Ali to Berlin to have lunch at the Kaefer."

But by now both knew that there had been no explosion at the Reichstag, but both also knew their information had been too late.

LANGLEY, VIRGINIA

Darned, Pistol Pete, the head of the CIA muttered as he paced his large office sipping a Diet Coke. Why are we always the last to know, why are we always one step behind, he questioned in his mind. Should I inform the President let her once again surmise that the CIA had failed. Already all the politicians on Capitol Hill had blamed his agency on the failures of international security, Iraq, Syria and more. But he knew these were not the failures of his CIA, his agency. It was the politicians' inability to act that created this mess, he thought. Yet, he had no choice and he picked up the telephone and called Monica Drew, the President of the United States.

I don't want to discuss it over the phone, Monica Drew had replied as Pistol Pete had begun the conversation.

"Get over here at once, come to the Oval Office," she had ordered.

Pistol Pete discarded his Diet Coke and went to his large closet where he kept several suits, dress shirts, ties and appropriate shoes. He undressed quickly, shedding his favorite apparel, blue jeans, a loose white Polo button down shirt and white sneakers. He knew Monica Drew despised blue jeans, she expected proper dress from all of her staff when they were about to meet with her.

CHAPTER XII

THE OVAL OFFICE, THE WHITE HOUSE

Monica Drew was not alone. Her Chief of Staff, Roger Kiefer, was sitting opposite her, facing the Commander in Chief. Neither got up as the head of the CIA, now dressed in a dark blue suit, white shirt, pin striped tie and black shoes, entered the office of the most powerful woman in the world.

Pistol Pete was not pleased to see Roger Kiefer, the chief of staff. Mr. Kiefer was always the first to blame the CIA, blame the agency for not providing the right information he needed to advise the President.

Monica Drew was not cordial, she had blamed much of her problems, her email scandals, her foundations problems, her foreign policy missteps on the poor information she had received from both the FBI and the CIA.

"Well," she said as soon as the head of the CIA entered her office, "tell me how you screwed up again."

"I am sorry," Pistol Pete responded, having difficulty controlling his emotions. "We did not screw up, but we received information from the Mossad I think I need to share with you."

"Why is it always information supplied to us by other intelligence agencies, why can't we be the first to know?" The President's chief of staff asked. He had not greeted the boss of the CIA, did not look at him as he asked the question.

"In my business, the spy business, we all work together, share information. At times our allies know first what is going on, at other times we do," Pistol Pete replied trying to calm his temper.

"Well, tell me the last time we had the info first?" Roger Kiefer asked as he smiled at his boss, the President.

"Enough", Monica Drew interjected. "Let's not argue, just tell us what is going on."

"OK," the head of the CIA began. "The whole issue is about Brexit."

"Brexit?" the President of the USA asked.

"Yes, Brexit," Pistol Pete continued, "I am sure you have been well informed, and understand what Brexit means to our country."

"Yes," Monica Drew lied, for she knew little about Brexit, its implications, how it could shift the balance of power.

The President's chief of staff snickered, he had tried to explain it all to his Commander –in-Chief. But he knew that her knowledge on the subject was no greater than that of the man on the street. Probably less, he thought with a smile.

"Madame President," Pistol Pete continued, "we now have evidence that Hezbollah tried to assassinate the President of the European Union."

"Why would they want to do that?" Monica Drew asked.

"Well, for them it would be like 911," he almost asked if she knew about that strike, but he did not. "It would be a major victory for them. But the CIA does not think that Hezbollah sponsored it, we think it was someone else."

"Who?" Monica Drew asked, now curious.

"As you know," CIA's chief continued, "Brexit is a major issue in Great Britain. A slim majority of the British people voted for it, voted to leave the European Union. But now there are second thoughts, many want Britain to rejoin, many believe that leaving the E.U. will destroy their economy."

"Who are the many?" the President asked.

"First of all, the royal family wants to stay out of the E.U., restore Britain to what it has once been. And that is how the current Prime Minister gained power. It was strictly a political move, she well knows Britain cannot survive outside of the E.U. But she sensed that many of the British people sided with the royal family, no longer did they want to be third in Europe, and have France and Germany dictate everything."

"OK, I get it, who in Britain wants their country back in the E.U.?" the President wanted to know.

"Many of Britain's lawmakers want it. They now realize it was a mistake. The effort to get back into the E.U. is spearheaded by Theresa Watson, the head of MI6, the Special Intelligence Service of Britain."

"Why don't the British people just have another referendum, a new vote?" Monica Drew, now better understanding the issue, asked.

"Even if the Brits want to get back into the E.U, the E. U won't let them."

"Why?" the President asked.

"The President of the E.U., Prince Wilhelm von Hohenzollern, is dead set against it. He never wanted Britain to be part of it. He believes Britain is not part of Europe, and to be fair, Britain has been a very difficult partner, always asking for special concessions."

"All right, I see it," Monica Drew continued. "How does it affect us, and the balance of power in the world?"

"Now, Madame President, you have a good grasp on the situation," her Chief of Staff interjected.

"Thank you," the President of the USA responded sarcastically. She never liked the sly remarks of the chief of staff who always thought he was smarter than anyone else. But her husband had insisted on his appointment.

"We at the CIA have good reason to believe that Russia is involved."

"Russia?" she asked in disbelief.

"Yes, Russia, the President of the Russian Federation wants to keep Britain out of the E.U., weaken it. As a Matter of fact we know that Russia bribed many of the English lawmakers to vote for Brexit. Russia spent millions of dollars, and their agents are already working in many of the 28 E.U. countries to have them leave Brexit, Greece leaving, appears to be next. A weak E.U., or better a no E.U., will mean a very strong Russia."

"That is a real threat to our country," Monica Drew exclaimed, "why did you not inform me?" she asked her Chief of Staff.

"I did," he responded nonchalantly, "but you seemed not to be interested."

"Tomorrow morning, at precisely 7 a.m., I want the entire security council in my office, and, Pete, I want you here as well."

CHAPTER XIII

SOCHI, RUSSIA

He knew he had made a mistake, a mistake he got away with. President Pavlov, the President of the Russian Federation, rested on his favorite beach in Sochi, Russia. He was clad only in his favorite Speedo bathing suit, letting the waves cover his muscular body. President Pavlov loved lying on the beach, close to the water where only the last waves would cover his body. He did not mind the wet sand, he loved to be covered by it.

Today the beach was empty, the season had just passed. Only a dozen security agents, all FSB, the former KGB, all dressed in black, surrounded him. He loved his men, trusted them, had groomed many when he was the leader of the KGB, and his men loved him, would die for him, he had no doubt.

His plan was straight forward, a weak E.U. meant a strong Russia and to keep Britain out of the E.U. was the first step, a very important one. He understood that Prince Wilhelm was a key player, one who would keep Britain out of the E.U. Pavlov had spent millions of dollars bribing all the British politicians to have Britain leave the E.U., the cornerstone of his plan. But he knew that Prince Wilhelm was key. He had to keep the Prince alive at all costs. It was only luck he thought, as he got up and took the large towel handed to him by one of his security guards, lucky that a rogue group of assassins, Hezbollah, failed to kill the Prince.

As President Pavlov dried himself on the beach of the Black Sea he made a decision. He would send six of his best agents to protect the President of the European Union. For his plan to succeed the E.U. President had to be kept alive. At least for now.

BERLIN, GERMANY

Nicole was already there. She had ordered room service to bring lunch to their suite on the sixth floor of the Regent Hotel. Nicole knew Adam would arrive soon, he had called her, asked her to have lunch in their suite. As soon as Adam arrived Nicole asked Adam about the meeting with Prince Wilhelm, but all Adam wanted was to have a Wiener Schnitzel for lunch. He would tell her all about the meeting later, after he enjoyed his favorite meal.

LONDON, 85 ALBERT EMBANKMENT, VAUXHALL, LAMBATH, HEADQUARTERS OF MI6

Theresa Watson, the first female chief of MI6, received the news at once. Hezbollah had failed to kill the Chancellor of Germany. Somehow, she was not surprised. She always wanted her people to do the job. But her Chief of Staff had convinced her it would be a mistake. There could be no direct link to Britain's intelligence agency and Hezbollah almost always succeeded. Not this time, she thought in dismay.

She got out of the plush leather chair behind her large desk and walked towards the window overlooking the river Thames. She reminisced. She had been the first woman to be appointed to head the agency by the Foreign Secretary, her boss. The Secret Intelligence Service or SIS, commonly known as MI6, Military Intelligence, Section 6, is the British intelligence agency supplying her government with foreign intelligence. Although it was created in 1907 to particularly focus on the activities of Germany, the existence of SIS and its chief was not officially acknowledged until 1992. Its first director was Captain Sir George Mansfield Smith-Cumming, who signed all of his correspondence with his initial "C" and always in green ink. It was a tradition all directors of MI6 have followed since.

The SIS chief is always appointed by and held accountable to the Foreign Secretary of Britain. The chief is the only member of SIS whose identity is officially made public. Traditionally most chiefs had been appointed from the various branches of the Military, but more recently chiefs have been career officers, and Theresa Watson was one of them. She had served in Her Majesty's Service for more than 20 years. Now Theresa Watson was uncertain of what to do next. She had no plan "B". She needed to consult with her Chief of Staff.

BERLIN, GERMANY

As soon as the Chancellor of Germany, Prince Wilhelm returned to his office at the Chancellery, he called the head of the BND, the Bundesnachrichtdienst, Germany's foreign intelligence agency. He asked for an immediate meeting. Prince Wilhelm wanted to know why his security had not detected the threat on his life, why a trained assassin from the U.S. seemed to be more informed about his security. And he wanted to inform his head of the BND that he had hired Adam Bergman to protect him.

LONDON, ENGLAND, 10 DOWNING STREET

Margaret Sawyer, the Prime Minister, also was informed that there had been an attempt to kill the Chancellor of Germany. The phone call had come from the head of MI6, Theresa Watson. It was a brief message, a message that informed the head of the British government, that Hezbollah had attempted to kill the Chancellor of Germany. Margaret Sawyer was not surprised, she knew that all heads of western governments were always a target. Someday it would be her, Margaret thought. But she did not know that it was her country, her secret service agency, which had planned the assassination of Germany's chancellor.

BEIRUT, LEBANON

"Ali, Ali, my love, how did you miss?" Hassan Nasral, the Secretary General of Hezbollah, asked his grandson as they both embraced in the deep bunker in south Beirut.

"I didn't," Ali replied, "all the players were not there. The Brits gave us bad information."

The old man smiled. He knew the Westerners could never be trusted.

"My mistake," he responded. "I trusted the information from the men, the British agents. I should have known better. I will never make that mistake again. And you should also learn, the Westerners are all infidels, cannot be trusted, need to be killed."

"I agree," Ali responded as he took a seat on the floor in his grandfather's bunker, a seat on the luxurious Persian carpet.

"From now on we will only follow Allah's wish, ignore the infidels, we surely cannot trust them."

"Please, grandpa, what is next for me? I want to serve Allah, I want to die, and meet the 70 virgins in heaven."

"Patience, my son," the old, wise man responded, "there will be a mission for you, one Allah has designed."

CHAPTER XIV

TEL AVIV, ISRAEL

The phone rang as he had just left his shower in the Dafner building, the headquarters of the Mossad, Israel's intelligence agency. He was naked, still wet as he exited the shower. The call was on his secure line, the line to the chief of the CIA.

"Maza, can you hear me?" Pistol Pete, the head of the CIA asked.

"Yes, clearly. What's up?"

"We have new information I want to share with you," Pistol Pete continued. "There was an attempt to kill the chancellor of Germany, the President of the E.U., an attempt by Hezbollah. The Secretary General of Hezbollah had sent his grandson to the Kaefer, he wore a suicide bomb. But he never pulled the trigger, his target, Germany's chancellor, never showed up."

"Interesting," Maza, the head of the Mossad, replied, feigning surprise. Maza had been well informed by his people, and he also knew that the attempt was not orchestrated by Hezbollah. After all his agency has more than 2000 sayanim working in London alone. A sayanim is not Mossad, but a helper, a volunteer, always 100% Jewish. Never would they refuse to perform a task if asked by the Mossad. As a result Maza always knew what went on at Whitehall. He knew the workings of the British Government better than the Prime Minister of Britain, he snickered. And he now also knew that the plot to kill the Chancellor of Germany was not a Hezbollah plan, it had been designed by MI6.

"Thank you for the information, keep me informed," he said as he hung up his phone. He dressed quickly in one of his usual attire, black pants, and dark brown sandals. He was late for the meeting with his staff.

BERLIN, GERMANY

The head of the BND, Germany's Bundesnachrichtdienst, was upset. The phone call from his boss, the chancellor, had been brief. Klaus Henzel detected that his boss was upset, there was a tone of irritation in his voice. He knew he needed to get to the chancellor as soon as possible.

The new headquarters of the BND, located on the Chausseestrasse, was only a short walk away. The headquarters was a magnificent building, one of Germany's largest administrative buildings, 5000 rooms housing more than 400 employees. Although the walk was short it was one of the longest walks Klaus had ever taken. He really did not want to rush, hear the bad news, yet he had to. His boss was waiting. Four BND agents accompanied him. As he rushed towards the chancellery, Klaus reminisced. He recalled how he had overseen the move of BND's headquarters from Pallach near Munich. How he had been the architect of BND's new location. It had taken several years but now his agency, his BND, CASCOPE was CIA's code name, was able to house all of his intelligence agencies here. A feat, he knew, no one would ever credit him for.

When he entered the chancellery, he did not have to wait. Prince Wilhelm was anxious to see him.

10 DOWNING STREET

Margaret Sawyer, the newly elected Prime Minister of Great Britain, also wanted information. She had been informed about the ill-fated attempt to kill the Chancellor of Germany. She needed to know why, who attempted it. Just another terrorist act by Hezbollah, or was there more?

She summoned Theresa Watson for a meeting at 10 Downing Street, surely Theresa would have all the answers. After all, Margaret thought my Secret Intelligence Service was one of the best, actually the best she thought with typical British arrogance. Margaret Sawyer had never fancied the idea of having her Foreign Secretary appoint a woman to head MI6. Not that anyone had ever thought Theresa Watson was not qualified, on the contrary, Theresa had an impeccable record as a career MI6 officer. No, that was not the reason. Was it because she wanted no other woman in her government with such power? No she thought, there was something about Theresa, Margaret Sawyer was not sure of what, that troubled her. Nonetheless, the Foreign Secretary had decided to appoint Theresa Watson as the head of MI6 and Margaret had to deal with it.

When Theresa Watson entered the office Margaret Sawyer immediately had the same reaction, the reaction she had when her Foreign Secretary had first introduced her. She could not quite put her finger on it, but something troubled her.

"Theresa," she said cordially, "thank you for coming."

"My pleasure, Madame Prime Minister." Theresa responded. "I am all yours."

"I want to get to the point, tea?" the Prime Minister asked.

"Yes, how kind of you," the head of MI6 responded.

"Please, let's sit on the couch, I have been sitting behind my desk too long," the Prime Minister instructed as she pointed towards the large leather couch in front of her desk.

"We will be more comfortable there."

Both took a seat on one of the two couches which were placed around a large cocktail table. Neither took a seat next to each other, both faced each other, directly looking into their eyes.

"Theresa", the Prime Minister began. "This whole affair in Berlin, this failed attempt by Hezbollah, it bothers me. I have this gut feeling there is more to it. Can you help?"

"We are on top of this," the head of MI6 replied without hesitation. "It clearly was an attempt by Hezbollah, another terrorist attack to fuel their cause. We know that the Secretary General of Hezbollah, Hassan Nasral, sent his grandson with a suicide bomb. No doubt, just another terrorist attempt."

The Prime Minister of Britain listened closely, looked the head of her secret intelligence service straight in the eye. She did not believe one word, she knew Theresa was lying.

"Thank you," Margaret Sawyer replied. "You know I had to make sure. Thank you for coming."

Neither had touched the tea that had been presented to them.

"My pleasure," the head of MI6 responded, "I am always at your service."

As Theresa Watson left the P.M.'s office, Margaret knew she had lied. The P.M. of Britain had a unique aptitude, she always knew when she was lied to. Margaret Sawyer returned to her desk carrying a cup of tea, the tea she had never shared with the head of her MI6. She sat down in the large leather chair still holding her cup. She took a sip, now it was but luke warm. She did not mind, she loved tea, hot, cold or just warm. But now she realized she had a problem. Clearly, she did not trust the head of MI6, Theresa Watson. She was convinced she was lying. How to find out the truth, she thought. The truth, she was convinced, would never be found within MI6, Theresa Watson controlled it.

The Prime Minister of Britain, Margaret Sawyer, had to find a person not part of MI6, another spy, one she could hire to get to the truth. And she needed the best.

CHAPTER XV

BERLIN, GERMANY

"That was one of the best schnitzels I ever had," Adam exclaimed as he pushed aside the plate and took another drink of the white wine. "Excellent," he said, "just the best."

"You were probably very hungry," Nicole said with a smile as she poured herself another glass of Pinot Grigio, one of Adam's favorite wines.

"You are right, I was hungry, and all that happened today was wonderful. You were right, meeting the Prince was the best idea you ever had, now I think we are safe, off the hook."

"Don't you think you have to tell me all about it? First of all, it was my idea, secondly, my ass was also on the line as well."

"Of course," Adam replied, "and you have the best ass, I will never ever let anything happen to it." He said as he laughed. "Everything worked out just as you predicted. The Prince understood, knows I am a professional killer, that I will kill for whoever pays me. But we had a long conversation. He explained the role of the E.U., why it is important to survive, how Russia is trying to destroy it to gain European dominance, how Mr. Pavlov, the President of the Russian

Federation, paid off all the British lawmakers to vote for Brexit. It was the best and most informative conversation I ever had."

"O.K.," Nicole responded, taking another sip of her wine, "where do we go from here?"

"Let me finish, please," Adam said. "I and the Prince knew nothing about the assassination attempt until I got back from the Spreewald. By then his security people had informed him about it. He was told it was an attempt by Hezbollah. But his head of the BND, Klaus Henzel, told him he had more information, information he did not want to share until we returned to the Reichstag. The Prince instructed Klaus to drive him directly to the chancellery, to come to his office and have me accompany him. Clearly the head of the BND was uncomfortable about it, he did not want me there. But the Prince insisted.

"What happened next?" Nicole was anxious to know.

"Well," Adam continued, "the three of us, the Prince, I and Klaus, the head of the BND, all met in the office of the Chancellor of Germany."

"Adam, please, don't drag it on, don't tease me," Nicole interrupted.

"It was then that Klaus told the Prince that the assassination attempt was designed by MI6, British intelligence. They had used Hezbollah as a cover."

"MI6? Why does MI6 want to kill the Prince?"

"It is the same reason why they had hired me to kill the Prince. MI6, at least the head of MI6, Theresa Watson, is convinced the Prince will never let Britain back into the E.U. She fanatically believes for her country to survive economically it has to reenter the E.U. Clearly eliminating the Prince will help that cause."

"Kill the Prince to get back in the E.U.?" Nicole asked

"Yes, that is MI6's plan. But not only theirs."

"What do you mean, not only theirs?"

"Nicole, I know we have talked about it before. It really is Mr. Pavlov, the President of the Russian Federation, who is orchestrating it all. He is using MI6 as a puppet. But now the Prince understands it all. He wants to cut all evil off at its source."

"What does that mean?" Nicole asked.

"Well, first," Adam continued, "the Prince knows that Russia is behind it all, it is the cause of all evil. MI6, or better, Theresa Watson, is just being used by the Russians. We need to let Russia erroneously think we are convinced that MI6 caused the attack."

"How do you do that?" Nicole asked.

"Simple," Adam replied, "you kill the head of MI6."

"Kill the head of MI6? Are you kidding? Who is going to do that?"

"You and I," Adam replied with a smile.

"All right, continue," Nicole asked. "So just theoretically we have killed the head of MI6, a task by the way, that is impossible. Then what?"

"Honey," Adam replied, "in our business the word impossible does not exist. But fair enough, I'll paint the rest of the picture."

Adam had now poured another glass of wine and walked back and forth in the large sitting room of his suite in the Regent Hotel.

"O.K.," Adam said, "let's continue to fantasize. The head of MI6 is dead, who shot her? Much speculation. The Prince in retaliation? That is what the Russians will conclude, that is what the Prince wants them to think. Now Mr. Pavlov will be confident that his plot to destroy the E.U. will succeed, that no one suspects it was he who pulled all the strings."

"Is it possible that she was killed for other than political reasons? Perhaps a lover, I understand she is not married," Nicole interjected.

"You mean a female lover?" Adam asked.

"A female?" Nicole questioned with raised eyebrows. "Why a female?"

"Because Theresa Watson is a Lesbian."

"A lesbian?" Nicole exclaimed in disbelief.

"As sure as I am Adam Bergman," he replied, smiling, "and that is why it is not impossible to assassinate her. That will allow us to get close to her, well, not us, but you."

Now Adam had a full grin on his face as he leaned forward and kissed Nicole on the cheek.

"What are you implying?" Nicole asks and now begins to see Adam's plan.

"We'll talk about those details later, but not now," Adam continued as he sat next to Nicole on the large white sofa in the living room of their suite.

"The Prince's plan to kill the head of MI6 is brilliant. He fully understands that it is the President of the Russian Federation, Mr. Pavlov, who wants to destroy the E.U... Britain is only his first step. By killing the head of MI6, Britain's attempt to reenter the E.U. will be greatly weakened, perhaps made impossible."

"I understand," Nicole responded.

"Why doesn't he kill the Chief of MI6?"

"Good question," Adam replied. "He probably has plans to do so. But the Prince wants to beat him to the punch. After all, to him it is personal. MI6 tried to kill him, Nicole," Adam continued, "let's pack our bags and go back to Capri. I need some rest. In three days, the Prince wants me back in Berlin to hear our plan to kill the Chief of MI6."

"Bags are ready to go," Nicole said, "I knew you were ready to go back home. But what happens after the assassination of SIS' chief?"

"Then," Adam said with a wide grin, we will face the real challenge."

"What is that?"

"To keep Britain out of the E.U. is not only what the Prince wants, but Mr. Pavlov as well. But it is only a piece of the Russian leader's plan, he wants all countries to leave the E.U."

"A Euro exits?" Nicole asked

"Yes," Adam replied, "the Prince calls it Eurexit, that's how Mr. Pavlov intends to make Russia great once again, to use a quote of America's former candidate for the office of the Presidency of the U.S.A."

"How does the Prince intend to stop him?" Nicole was eager to find out.

"Simple," Adam replied, "he wants us to kill him. Another challenge and you know how much I love challenges."

CHAPTER XVI

CAPRI, ITALY

Nicole and Adam had arrived in the early evening, then had enjoyed a quick dinner in their apartment which Adam had prepared. Both were tired and needed a good night's rest. But Adam wanted more, he wanted to make love. Their love making was short by Adam's standards. It was one hour of bliss, one hour during which Nicole had several orgasms. Adam was patient, he waited until the last minute.

Adam did not sleep well, he had too much on his mind. He arose at 6 a.m., dressed in his Nike jogging attire and went for his customary 6 mile run on his beautiful island. When he returned Nicole was still asleep. He took a long shower letting hot water relax his body, relax his mind. As he left the shower his telephone ran and Adam rushed towards it not wanting the phone to interrupt Nicole's sleep.

It was the concierge of his apartment building.

"Sir, sorry I am calling so early, he said in Italian, "but there is a gentleman in the lobby he wants to see you. He said it is urgent."

"No need to apologize," Adam responded, "I will be in the lobby in 10 minutes. Please ask the gentleman to wait."

"Gracie," was the response from the concierge.

Adam dressed quickly, white linen slacks, a white linen shirt and sandals. When Adam entered the lobby of his apartment building, he saw the man standing by the concierge desk. Clearly a Brit, Adam surmised, dressed in a dark blue pin striped suit, white button-down shirt, a light blue tie and black oxford shoes.

"Good morning," Adam said as he extended his right hand to meet his guest.

"Good morning," the man from Britain replied as he gave Adam a firm handshake.

"Sorry for the intrusion so early in the morning, but it is a matter of importance I need to talk to you about."

"No apologies needed, I always get up early," Adam responded with a smile. "What can I do for you?"

"If you don't mind," the Brit said," could we take a stroll? What I have to say is rather confidential."

"Of course. Let's take a walk. It is a beautiful day and no better place to take a stroll than in Capri."

Both men entered the street and walked down Via Camerelle, neither spoke. After several minutes the man from Britain broke the silence.

"My name is Sir Winston Blackburn. I am the chief of staff of the Prime Minister of Britain. She sent me to speak with you. You must understand that this conversation is confidential, not a word can be repeated. As a matter of fact, I have never come to Capri. Another man on my staff, using my identity, is traveling to Vienna today. But I know you are a professional, you will honor my request."

"Of course," Adam replied.

"I'll be brief and right to the point, if you don't mind," the British man continued.

"No, I don't mind. This is the way I like it." Adam said, already liking the man.

"All right, here it is," the chief of staff of Britain's Prime Minister continued, "my boss is upset about the failed assassination attempt on the German chancellor. Rumor has it that Britain was responsible but used Hezbollah as a front. I can assure you that my Prime Minister had no knowledge of it, but she wants to know who did it."

Adam feigned surprise. "Surely you have one of the best intelligence agencies in the world, MI6. Why not have them investigate it?"

"That is where the problem lies," Sir Winston continued. My boss does not trust the chief of MI6. The Prime Minister wants an independent to look into it, and she wants the best."

"She does not trust the head of her own foreign intelligence office?" Adam asked, again feigning surprise.

"Well let's not get into that. That is another matter. She has determined that you are the best person for the job, she wants you to find out. And we are willing to pay well for the information. I have been authorized to pay you 10 million pounds."

10 million pounds for information Adam already knew. Information the head of Germany's secret service, the BND, had shared with him and Prince Wilhelm only a day ago at Germany's chancellery. An easy 10 million pounds.

"It won't be easy, it will take some time, but I will do it," Adam responded.

"Very well," the Brit said. "Give me your wiring information. The money will be deposited into your bank account this afternoon. We trust you, we know you have a reputation to protect."

The Prime Minister's chief of staff stopped abruptly, shook Adam's hand.

"A pleasure meeting you. I think my boss made the right choice."

Adam stood still as he watched the Brit walk away to hail a cab back to Marina Grande, to catch the ferry boat back to Naples. Then Adam turned and walked back to his apartment. He could not wait to tell Nicole. Now he had two heads of state who had employed him. Would there be a third he wondered as he smiled?

PARADISE ISLAND, BAHAMAS

Prince Wilhelm had rented all the villas at the Ocean Club, not really he, but a wealthy German industrialist, a close friend of the Prince. They did not meet at one of the meeting rooms at the fashionable hotel. Instead, they met on the beach. A small tent had been erected there, it contained a small table and several chairs, beach chairs. A small party for tourists, no doubt, any passerby would surmise. But security was tight. BND, and AWA, Abwehramt, agents of the Austrian intelligence force, and private guards from Madrid, protected the tent. No one was in clear sight, all just tourists on the white sand beach. The food, fresh shrimp, lobster, tuna, swordfish, all was delivered to the tent by waiters, waiters from the BND.

All were in attendance, all the people Prince Wilhelm had asked to be there, the new chancellor of Austria, the Grand Duke of Russia and his father, and, of course, Adam and Nicole. But they had not been invited to the tent. Prince Wilhelm had asked them to be close, to protect his meeting place.

"Clearly, if Russia becomes part of the E.U.," Prince Wilhelm began as all had been served Cristal Champagne, "there will be no Eurexit, then there will be a true balance of power in the world."

"How do we get Russia to join the E.U.?" the young Grand Duke asked, knowing it could never happen.

"Now that is the key," Prince Wilhelm answered, "now you need to trust my judgment."

All were silent.

"If Mr. Pavlov is no longer a player, Russia does not have a strong successor, he made sure of it, he wants no challenge to his authority. Russia loves a strong leader, she doesn't mind an authoritative government, even dictatorship. In case of Mr. Pavlov's death the void of strong, authoritative leadership has to be filled immediately. The Russian people have watched in wonder what I have done, watched the resurgence of Germany as a great economic power, a power led by a Royal, a descendant of the House of Hohenzollern. Why reinvent the wheel, I believe the Russian people will think, why not follow Germany? Why not elect the direct descendant of the former Russian Czar, why not elect the Grand Duke as President of the Russian Federation? Of course, the politicians, the members of the Politburo will have other ideas. But surely, they all can be bribed, bribed more easily than Mr. Pavlov bribed the British lawmakers to vote for Brexit. It will take money, of course, but also the promise of appointments of key Russian lawmakers to important offices in the new government."

"Uncle," the Grand Duke replied enthusiastically, as he had carefully listened. "It could work."

"Father," he said as he turned to his father, what do you think?"

"Son," he replied with a broad smile on his face, "I have always told you that Wilhelm is a brilliant politician, a brilliant strategist."

"Thank you," Prince Wilhelm replied, trying to be humble. "The truth however, is that history has taught us that the better politicians are the Habsburgs." He smiled as he turned to face the Archduke of Austria

"What is your opinion?"

"Quite frankly, and I hate to admit it, now you have topped the Habsburgs, your plan is brilliant."

"I also want to hear what Baron von Rosenberg has to say, we need his input. Israel is as important as Russia, in my opinion. To bring the Middle East into our scheme is essential to make it successful. So please give us your thoughts, and please be frank, you will not offend anyone here, after all you are part of the family."

Israel's Premier felt uncomfortable. After all he was not a direct descendant of the European dynasty.

"First of all, I feel humbled and very grateful to have been invited to this meeting. Israel will never forget your graciousness, your consideration to make my country an integral part of it all. And I want to especially thank Prince Wilhelm for accelerating Israel's entry into the European Union as a full member."

CHAPTER XVII

SOCHI, RUSSIA

He loved riding bareback on his horse along the beach of his favorite resort, Sochi. And he always rode shirtless. Despite his age of 66 his body looked much younger, he was muscular, the build of an athlete. Sochi was the place he always came to, to relax, to plan. His time at the Kremlin was always occupied with administrative work, with local politics, with who to bribe next, with who stood in his way, needed to be eliminated.

Sochi was different. Here he could relax and think about the big picture, how to make Russia great again. There was no question in his mind he had to disassemble the European Union. The union had always been a thorn in his side, without the E.U. Russia would be great again. And he knew that Britain's exit from the E.U. was key. It was the first step in his plan of Eurexit, of all the E.U. nations leaving the union. And he had succeeded. Yes, it had cost him dearly, the British lawmakers were not cheap, it took millions of American dollars to bribe them. But dollars were only a small price to pay for his mother Russia to become a world power again.

Yet, he was concerned. The British who had been a key to the first step in his plan to destroy the E.U., were having second thoughts.

Particularly it was the head of Britain's foreign intelligence agency, MI6, who was determined to make Britain once more a member of the E.U. He needed to do all he could to stop her, a woman, he thought in disdain. No woman would stop his plan, his millions of dollars he had spent to make Russia what she had once been. Of course, his secret service, the FSB, previously known as the KGB, the agency he once headed, was capable of eliminating Theresa Watson, the chief of MI6. But he wanted no trace back to him, all needed to know that Russia had no interest in the affairs of the E.U. His secret service, the FSB, Federal Security Service, had informed him that Prince Wilhelm, Germany's chancellor, planned to assassinate the chief of MI6. President Pavlov, however, never put his chips on one number. He decided he needed a backup in case the Prince failed.

He needed a plan "B". Clearly it could be none of his men, none of his six agents he had sent to protect Prince Wilhelm. No, he thought, it could be no one from his security agency, the FSB. He had to recruit an independent killer, a professional. He thought about the terrorists, Al Qaeda, Hezbollah, they certainly were a choice. But they were fanatics, not professionals. The President of the Russian Federation was a perfectionist, he only believed in the best. Only the best could make Russia great again.

LONDON, 10 DOWNING STREET

"Thank you for the call," the Prime Minister of Great Britain answered Adam's call, "I would have never expected it."

"I am certain," Adam reassured her, "it was the head of your Secret Intelligence Agency, your MI6 division, who planned it all. She is determined to have Britain re-enter the European Union. It was a pleasure doing business with you. Please call me if you need my services again."

"Thank you for all you have done," the PM of Great Britain replied. As you requested the fee has been transferred into your Cayman account per your request. Hopefully we will never need your services again." She was wrong!

Then a clique, the call was over. The Prime Minister now knew she had much to worry about, the demand of her people to rejoin the European Union. But first she had to take care of Theresa Watson, Chief of MI6.

It took Margaret Sawyer, the PM of Great Britain, less than 30 minutes to change her mind. Clearly her chief of MI6 had to be eliminated in order to stop her efforts to reenter the EU. Margaret also knew the assassination could not be carried out by anyone even remotely close to her, but by a foreigner, a trained assassin. She called for her trusted Chief of Staff and explained what she had learned from Adam and asked for his advice. The Chief of Staff did not hesitate for but a minute.

"Madame Prime Minister," he replied, "it is clear you are right, It has to be done by the best, I will call Adam Bergman at once."

CAPRI, ITALY

Adam knew that he and Nicole had to return to Berlin in a couple of days. But Adam needed to relax, and develop the plan to assassinate the chief of MI6.

Victorino, the captain of the gozzo, a replica of the old working boats on Capri, met Nicole and Adam at Marina Piccola, the small marina on Capri, only a short, steep downhill walk from Adam's apartment.

Nicole and Adam often took the boat ride around the island with Victorino. The small boat was always well supplied, wine, fresh vegetables from Victorino's garden and she urchins, Adam's favorite food.

Adam and Nicole were clad only in their bathing suits and relaxed on the large sun pad at the bow of the boat. The gozzo left Marina Piccola and lazily pushed into the Mediterranean Sea. The waves splashed gently into the wooden hull, the sun was bright, the sea calm. This is where Adam liked to plan, no one to disturb his mind, none but the gentle waves. That's when he developed his plan to assassinate the chief of MI6. He considered many options, Nicole getting close to the lesbian chief, a long-range rifle shot and many more.

But, as he relaxed on the large, comfortable pad on the front deck of the gozzo, he had another idea. Why not have Hezbollah do it? Why not have the chief of MI6 and the chancellor meet at the Kafer, the restaurant at the Reichstag building.

Of course, the Prince could not be there, Adam had to protect him. But would Hezbollah miss the opportunity to kill the chief of MI6? He did not think so. Once before Hezbollah had failed to pull the trigger, this time, Adam gambled, they would not fail.

"Nicole", Adam exclaimed as he rolled over on the launch pad of the gozzo and faced Nicole.

"Good news for you, I changed my mind."

"Changed your mind?" Nicole asked as she removed her sunglasses to look him in the eye.

"Yes, I have decided that you do not have to go to bed with the lesbian chief of MI6 and kill her."

"How kind of you, I never intended to have sex with a spymaster. Well, that's not true, I do like sex with some spies, the tall and muscular ones." Nicole responded leaning over and kissed Adam on the mouth. "But what is your alternative, what is your plan?"

"Naturally we can leave no trace back to the Prince." Adam continued as he left the sun pad to walk aft and retrieve another bottle of Pinot Grigio from Victorino's well stacked cooler.

"So the perfect plan is to have someone far removed from us and the Prince do it," he said as he walked back to the bow of the gozzo.

"Please hand me your glass and I'll pour you some wine."

Nicole reached for her glass and handed it to him.

"Thank you, please continue," she was anxious to learn about her lover's plan.

"I think Hezbollah is our best choice. They would love the publicity of killing two very important people," Adam continued. He now sat back on the sun pad of the gozzo and took a large sip of his wine.

"How can we pull that off, how can we induce Hezbollah to do it?" Nicole asked.

"Now that part is easy," Adam answered. "I can call my friend, Maza, the head of Mossad and ask a favor."

"What kind of favor?" Nicole was eager to know.

"To leak information to the Secretary General of Hezbollah, the Mossad has done it often when it benefited them."

"What kind of information?" Nicole, intrigued by Adam's plan, urged him on.

"Information regarding the meeting of the chief of MI6 and the chancellor of Germany in a public place, an opportunity for a perfect kill."

"Sounds like a good plan to me, beats me having to go to bed with the chief of MI6", Nicole responded.

"What is the right public place?" she continued.

"It is the Kaefer, the restaurant on top of the Reichstag building. Prince Wilhelm has lunch there every Tuesday and Thursday. For him to meet there with another dignitary would not seem out of the ordinary. But there is a potential problem." Adam said.

"What is it?" Nicole wanted to know

"The terrorists, Hezbollah, always want a massive kill, a bomb, a suicide vest. That helps their propaganda, makes bigger news. There is no way that the Prince wants any collateral damage, no other people killed, none of the buildings destroyed."

"Well, that sort of kills your plan," Nicole interrupted.

"Not quite," Adam said, "hear me out. When Maza instructs one of his double agents who has infiltrated Hezbollah, he needs to make it clear that the specific information regarding the time, the place and the security of the Prince's meeting is conditioned on one demand."

"What is that?"

"That the assassination has to be carried out with a rifle or a pistol shot, no bomb?"

"Why would Hezbollah oblige. They can agree, get all the information and then still use a bomb. As a matter of fact, I am sure they will use a bomb," Nicole emphatically replied.

"More wine?" Adam asked and poured Nicole another glass.

"Of course, you are right. That's why the Mossad agent needs another carrot for Hezbollah, a carrot the Secretary General cannot refuse to accept."

"What is that carrot?" Nicole asked.

"The juiciest of all. The chance to kill the President of the United States. The Mossad agent needs to assure if the kill in Berlin is clean, no bomb, no collateral damage, then Hassan Nasral will be given information that would allow him to kill the President of the USA."

"Do you think he will buy it?" Nicole asked, seriously doubting it.

"Probably not, but you never know," Adam replied.

"Then how do we make sure the hit in Berlin will be clean?" Nicole responded.

"Simple, obviously the Prince will never show up at the luncheon. Secondly, you and I will be there to make sure there is no bomb."

"Will there be a bomb?" Nicole asked nervously.

"Of course," Adam replied, "I never trust those terrorist bastards."

The first phone call Adam made from the public telephone as soon as he and Nicole had left Victorino's gozzo was brief. He called the chief of staff of the Prime Minister of Britain, and explained his plot to kill the head of MI6. The Prince and the chief of Britain's SIS needed to meet on the Prince's turf. The PM's chief of staff immediately agreed after Adam had explained more of the details of his plan. But Sir Winston needed the approval of his boss, his P.M.

"Please wait in the booth," Sir Winston asked, "I will call you right back."

The phone rang within minutes

"It is a go," was the message.

Adam made another call, a call to Tel Aviv, to his close friend Maza, head of the Mossad.

"Yes," Maza answered.

"It is Adam, I need a favor, actually the Prince, the Chancellor of Germany, needs it."

"OK, I'll do what I can," Maza responded.

"I will give you all the details later. But for now here is the bottom line. I need one of your double agents, one who has infiltrated Hezbollah, to leak information about a meeting between the head of MI6 and the chancellor of Germany. Can you do it?"

"Of course," Maza replied, "just let me know all the details."

Maza hung up his phone. He smiled. The head of the Mossad was well aware of the Prince's plan. After all his agents in the BND, Germany's Secret Service, kept him well informed. Maza and Israel had two reasons to support the chancellor of Germany. He was aware of Russia's plan to disassemble the E.U. and a strong Russia was not in the interest of Israel. In addition, his Prime Minister wanted Israel to join the E.U. as a full member. Although Israel had been an associate state of the European Union since 1995 it still was not part of the nine countries on the E.U. agenda for future enlargement.

In the past many European leaders, a former Italian Prime Minister, a Spanish Prime Minister, and more, had urged Israel to join. On an economic level Israel's relationship with the E.U. had been successful, but politically Israel perceived the E.U. to be pro-Palestinian in the Israel-Palestine conflict.

But Prince Wilhelm felt different. He was determined to bring Israel into the E.U. as a permanent member as soon as possible. After all, he always jokes, if Israel can be a full member of the UEFA, the Union of European Football Association, why should they not be a permanent member of the E.U.?

SOUTH BEIRUT, LEBANON

"My son," the Secretary General of Hezbollah, addressed his grandson, he always called him his son. They were close like father and son.

Both were sitting in the bunker in South Beirut, a bunker Hassan Nasral, the Secretary General of Hezbollah had not left in years. It was the Israeli drone strikes he feared, the reason he had not seen the sun in more than four years.

"Finally, we have found the perfect target for you. It will bring more joy to our people than 9-11. It is a gift from Allah. It is perfect."

Hassan was breathing heavily now, for his pancreatic cancer had spread to his lungs. He knew he would die soon. And when he was as near to his death as he could determine, he would leave his bunker to see the sun one last time, and to have the Israeli drones kill him.

"Please, grandpa, tell me all about it. You know I am ready. I will not fail you and I will not fail Allah," his young grandson proclaimed enthusiastically.

"Here it is," the old man responded in almost a whisper, breathing heavily. "The chief of MI6, Britain's intelligence agency and the Chancellor of Germany will meet at the Kaefer, the restaurant you have visited before."

"Yes," the young man replied, "I know the place well."

"The procedure will be the same. Your vest will be in the same toilet as before. Retrieve it, gradually, do not run, get as close to the table where the head of MI6 and the Chancellor will be having lunch. Then pull the trigger.

Remember, there is no need to get very close, your vest is full of explosives, it will blow most of the building into the sky. But be careful, security is tight. We have learned that not only MI6 agents will be there, but agents from Germany's BND, their secret service. But more importantly, the President of the Russian Federation has sent 6 of his best FSB men to protect the Chancellor of Germany."

The Secretary General of Hezbollah did not know about Nicole and Adam, information his agents had failed to uncover. And he did not tell him that he had been asked for a clean kill, not to use a bomb.

CHAPTER XVIII

MOSCOW, THE KREMLIN

The President of the Russian Federation, Vladimir Pavlov knew that the head of the MI6 needed to be eliminated. He also understood that there could be no link to Russia, and he knew to get it done he had to hire the best.

The six FSB agents he had sent to protect the Chancellor of Germany were well informed, knew about the luncheon meeting between the head of MI6 and the Chancellor of Germany, a meeting arranged by the Prime Minister of Great Britain.

Vladimir did not often drink alcohol in the middle of the day. But today he made an exception. He walked towards the rustic but elegant bar in his office and poured himself a vodka, a vodka on ice. He took the glass and paced his large office. He did not sit down, he always made his most important decisions while pacing, staying active. He believed it stimulated his blood stream, it let him think more clearly. The head of MI6 was an obstacle to his plan, his plan to destroy the European Union. She needed to be eliminated, he knew. Clearly his FSB agents were capable of doing it but he wanted no trace, no evidence that Russia had anything to do with it. He had to find someone else, a professional, a perfectionist like himself. Vladimir had heard of the assassin, the American, a former Navy Seal, trained by the best, the NSA and the Mossad. As he took a large drink from his favorite Vodka, he decided to hire Adam Bergman. Vladimir Pavlov had learned a lesson, a lesson he would never forget, a lesson that made him rise through the ranks of the KGB, the former Russian Intelligence agency, a lesson that got him to be the President of the Russian Federation. The lesson really was quite simple, he thought, know your friends but know your enemies even better. Vladimir decided he needed to meet with Adam Bergman, the man he wanted to hire to eliminate the Chief of MI6.

CAPRI, ITALY

Adam had just hung up the phone in the public booth on Capri Island, had just concluded his call to the Prime Minister of England, when the phone rang again. He hesitated for a moment, was the Prime Minister calling him again, did she have another question?

Adam decided to pick up the receiver, the voice had no British accent, it was clearly Russian.

"The President of the Russian Federation would like to meet with you, tomorrow, at the Berlin Brandenburg Airport in Schoenefeld. He is in Berlin to meet Germany's chancellor. There will be a car waiting for you on the tarmac, at Gate A30. Please be there, his plane lands at 10:32 a.m.

A click, no chance for Adam to respond. The opportunity to meet Vladimir Pavlov, the President of the Russian Federation, was a chance Adam would not miss. Vladimir Pavlov wanted to meet him, Adam thought in awe. In a way Adam almost admired the man, a man made of his own cloth, intelligent, an athlete, calculating, ruthless and a cold-blooded killer, but also a man who was a strong leader admired by his people.

Adam knew he had been followed by the FSB, Russia's intelligence agency. Two of the six men the Russian President had sent to Germany to protect Prince Wilhelm, to be closer to his enemies than his best friends, clearly knew the telephone number of the booth Adam was standing in.

Adam immediately picked up the telephone receiver and called NetJets, a private jet service he had joined several months ago. No problem, he was told, meet us at 7 a.m. at the airport, we will get you to Berlin on time.

BERLIN BRANDENBURG AIRPORT

The meeting was brief. Adam and Vladimir Pavlov sat in the back seat of the large Mercedes limousine. Several other vehicles surrounded their car, surely all FSB, Adam surmised. As soon as he entered the limousine of Russia's President, Vladimir Pavlov gave him a warm handshake and looked him straight into the eye.

"A pleasure meeting you," he said smiling. "I have heard much about you, but I wanted to meet you in person."

"My pleasure," Adam responded, not avoiding eye contact, "how can I help?"

"You are very astute," Vladimir Pavlov responded. "Yes, I need your help. I hear you are the best, a man who can be trusted, a professional, a perfectionist."

"Thank you for the compliment," Adam said, still looking directly into the blue eyes of Russia's leader.

"It is quite simple," the Russian leader continued, liking the man sitting next to him. "I have a job, one that takes the best. Of course, my people can do it, but I want no trace back to my Russia."

"Of course," Adam replied, "tell me what you want me to do."

Now Vladimir Pavlov knew that Adam was the right person. It did not take him long to study people, to know them, that he had learned years ago at the KGB.

"Adam," he continued, "I want you to assassinate the head of MI6 at the meeting in Berlin at the Kaefer," he continued. The head of Russia was always direct, never beating around the bush, that's how he had gained the highest office of his land.

"OK," Adam responded, "how much?"

Now Vladimir Pavlov knew he made the right choice. The man was direct, honest, straight forward, the kind of man he liked, the kind of man he trusted.

"Twenty million dollars, ten we will send into your account now if you agree, ten after the job."

"OK", Adam said as he reached for the handle of the back door of the limousine, "it is done."

There was no handshake, only an understanding between two men who were much alike. Adam left the limousine and strolled along the tarmac back to his private jet, not believing his fortune. Separate clients paying him handsomely for the same job, a job he personally would orchestrate, but never would he pull the trigger.

The President of the Russian Federation watched Adam as he left the limousine. He knew he had made the right choice. Unlike the Prime Minister of Great Britain, he knew he would ask for Adam's services again.

CHAPTER XIX

BERLIN, REICHSTAG BUILDING

It was a beautiful day in Berlin, in early October. The sky was blue, the sun shone high above, not a cloud in the sky. The Kaefer restaurant at the Reichstag building was buzzing with tourists, all asking for a table on the terrace. But much of the terrace had been cordoned off, no one was allowed to enter it. BND security forces made sure the terrace was off limits. Today it was reserved for the chancellor of Germany and his guest, the head of MI6.

But BND agents were not the only ones, MI6 too had sent its agents to protect their chief, and there were the FSB agents Mr. Pavlov had sent to protect Germany's chancellor.

Adam and Nicole had arrived at the Reichstag building early, several hours before the luncheon meeting of Prince Wilhelm was to take place.

Hezbollah had been instructed to make it a clean kill, no collateral damage, no bomb. Adam's instincts, instincts developed over many years, told him there was a bomb, not a bomb that would be detonated via a remote device or a cell phone. No, Adam was certain Hassan Nasrahl, the Secretary General of Hezbollah, had instructed his assassin to get close to the targets, to look into their eyes, to make sure of no mistake, not this time.

Adam and Nicole had searched for more than two hours, no bomb. Then Adam had the urge to urinate and he had to do it right away. He looked to his left and noticed the public toilet next to the entrance of the Kafer restaurant, only steps away, he also noticed the broad yellow tape stretched across the door of the toilet and the large sign, "closed, under construction". But Adam had to go, ignored the signage, stepped over the tape and entered the public bathroom. The toilet lid had been lowered and Adam used his left hand to raise it. Immediately he saw the black vest in the bowl which had been emptied of water, and he saw the handgun strapped to it. Never trust those terrorist bastards, he thought, as he retrieved the bomb vest. It took him less than one minute to disarm the bomb, then he swung the vest over his shoulder, but placed the gun back into the dry toilet bowl. Now you either play it my way or you don't play at all he thought with a grin. Then he relieved himself in the sink, the Beretta, the gun in the bowl had to stay dry. He left the toilet taking care to step over the yellow tape, leaving it undisturbed. As he reached the edge of the terrace of the Reichstag building he nonchalantly tossed the now harmless vest onto the porch below.

Adam leisurely entered the Kaefer restaurant, now he would wait, he knew the enemy would come. Adam had strapped his favorite gun, a Baretta, to the inside of his left ankle, his favorite spot. Security at the Reichstag had been instructed by the Chancellor himself, to let Adam carry a gun.

But Ali Nasrahl, the grandson of the Secretary of Hezbollah, had no such clearance. Ali also had made a reservation at the Kaefer restaurant, avoiding the long lines of tourists waiting to view the building of the Bunderstag.

As soon as Ali cleared security, he had been required to submit a copy of his passport days ahead, he entered the elevator which took him to the terrace of the Reichstag building. Ali was nervous now, he knew he could not fail, not disappoint his grandfather again, not fail Allah. But he also knew he had to remain composed. Ali waited until all the passengers in the elevator had left, most walking along the terrace of the building, a few entering the terrace restaurant.

Once Ali left the elevator he walked directly towards the toilet, the one he had visited not long ago. Again he stepped over the broad yellow tape exclaiming "closed, under construction," quickly opened the door and stepped into the public bathroom. Again he was surprised how clean it was, no debris on the floor. He quickly stepped towards the white bowl covered by its lid. Ali was anxious now, adrenaline rushing through his veins, his kill only minutes away. He kicked the lid open with his right foot and stared in disbelief, no vest, no bomb. What had gone wrong, he wondered. Should I again abort the mission? But then he saw the gun, a Baretta placed inside the dry toilet bowl. Now he knew what Allah wanted him to do.

Ali reached for the gun, examined it, made sure it was loaded, and tucked it into the back of his khaki trousers. Today was his moment to meet the 70 virgins in heaven.

He removed his belt and placed it on the sink, then he left the toilet, stepped over the tape and waved for the waiter standing near the entrance of the Kaefer restaurant. The waiter obliged after Ali told him he had dropped his Rolex watch in the toilet bowl, could he help him. Of course, the kind waiter responded. Both entered the public toilet and Ali reached for his belt he had readied in the sink and strangled the kind waiter. Quickly he removed his and the other man's clothing. His clothing he placed in the dry toilet bowl and set it on fire. He then tucked the Baretta in the back of his pants, not really his pants, but the pants of the dead waiter. Ali entered the Kaefer dressed as any of the other waiters. He walked towards the large counter of the restaurant behind which the food was prepared. He took two bottles of sparkling water and headed towards the terrace. He noticed all the security agents, and he saw the Chief of Britain's MI6, an older woman, all dressed in a black pants suit. How appropriate, Ali thought, black, the right dress for this occasion. But then he hesitated, he did not see the Chancellor of Germany, his other target. But Ali knew he could not fail again, he had to pull the trigger, kill the Chief of MI6, meet his 70 virgins, please Allah, please his grandfather.

Adam had observed it all. He had followed Ali as he left the elevator, watched him as he entered the toilet, watched him lure the Kaefer waiter into the bathroom, watched him exit the toilet dressed as one of Kaefer's waiters. Adam was patient. He then saw Ali retrieve the two bottles of water and approach the table of the Chief of MI6. No one stopped him. Adam noticed a hesitation, perhaps a second thought, but then Ali reached behind his back and pulled out the gun and shot the Chief of MI6 between the eyes. Adam had anticipated it, he already had his gun ready to fire when Ali reached for his Beretta. But Adam waited. He had a job to do, a job that paid well, paid for by more than one client. Then the bullet from his gun entered Ali's head, instantly killing the grandson of the Secretary General of Hezbollah.

Now there was chaos, turmoil, at the Kaefer. MI6 agents were covering the dead body of their chief, BND agents rushing Adam out of the restaurant Only the FSB agents, Mr. Pavlov's people, the ones he had sent to protect the Chancellor of Germany, left in no haste. All had gone according to plan. Mr. Pavlov would be pleased. Surely now they all deserved a Vodka.

CHAPTER XX

POTSDAM, SCHLOSS SANSSOUCI

For years Prince Wilhelm had not returned to the place where 250 years ago one of his forefathers had always found peace. But now he needed peace, peace of mind, peace to think clearly. The Prince decided to spend a week at the Schloss, walk the beautiful gardens, play the flute and even perhaps compose some music as Frederick the Great, King of Prussia, had done more than two and a half centuries ago. This is where his forefather had found peace of mind, where he seemed to have found the answer to the questions he then had sought. Prince Wilhelm hoped he could find the answers he needed.

Sanssouci is now a major world attraction, a world heritage site, visited by more than two million people from all over the world each year. But the German chancellery requested to close the Schloss and its extensive gardens to all tourists while the Prince occupied the palace. The Schloss is more like a chateau, containing only 10 principal rooms, and built on a terraced hill in the center of the park. Sanssouci's park was the main attraction of Federick's summer palace, Prince Wilhelm always thought. He loved the vineyard, the thousands of fruit trees, the greenhouses and nurseries, the expansive meadows, the fountains as well as the temples and trellises erected in the same rococo style at the palace. It all gave the grounds a feeling of tranquility, a haven of no worry.

The Prince had decided to occupy the former King's apartments composed of an audience room, a music room, a study, a library, a long gallery and the bedroom. His staff occupied the guest rooms adjourning the Marble Hall, one of the principal halls at the entrance area.

Shortly after his late afternoon arrival Prince Wilhelm decided to take a stroll and left the palace. He stood outside of the chateau and overlooked the terraced vineyard in front of him.

Yes, he thought, all had gone according to plan, the plan Adam Bergman had designed. The chief of MI6, his target to avoid Britain reentering the European Union, had been eliminated, and there was no trace that led to him. As a matter of fact, Hezbollah enthusiastically took credit for the kill. One of their greatest victories, no Allah's victory, the General Secretary of Hezbollah had proclaimed. Now the Prince needed to take care of the true cancer which tried to kill his European Union. This task, he realized, would be far more difficult. He needed Adam Bergman.

Then one of his security agents approached him, there was a call, a call from Madrid, Spain. It was important the agent said, it was from a family member.

Prince Wilhelm never refused a call from a member of his family. But Madrid, who could that be? He quickly walked back to the Schloss. He took the phone call in one of the entrance halls to the Schloss. The phone had been secured by the BND, his security agency.

"Wilhelm, it is me, Prince Klaus. "

"Prince Klaus?" Wilhelm tried to recall.

"Yes," the man answered. "I am calling from Madrid, you and I have the same birthdate, we are family. Did you receive the flowers I sent you when you were hospitalized at the Charitee Hospital?"

Now the Prince recalled. Years ago he had been shot, recuperated at the place of his birth, the famous Charitee Hospital in Berlin. He had received many bouquets of flowers, but one stood out. It had an inscription, one he would never forget, "Truth not belief will prevail."

Now Prince Wilhelm knew who had sent the flowers, who was calling him now. It was the father of the direct claimant to the headship of the Imperial Family of Russia, the father of the Grand Duke George Miklailovich of Russia, a member of the Holstein Gottorp-Romanov family, a member of his family.

Although in 1917 the Bolshovists had destroyed the Romanovs, the second dynasty to rule over Russia, they managed to kill 18 members, 407 survived and had gone into exile.

"Please, let me get to the reason for my call. My son, the true heir to Russia's throne, has been very active in the European Union. He is a strong supporter of your ideas, he would like to meet again, get more involved, help you anyway he can. Discuss all the details."

"Of course," Prince Wilhelm responded without hesitation. "I am at your service. Family means everything to me."

"Let's meet somewhere in private, somewhere we can be alone, just family."

"No problem," the chancellor of Germany replied. "I know the perfect place."

"OK," the voice from Madrid responded, "please set it up, can't wait to see you again."

CHAPTER XXI

THE WHITE HOUSE, WASHINGTON, D.C.

It was her day. Only days ago, she had become the most powerful person in the world, the President of the United States of America, the first woman ever to do so. It had been a tough fight, a struggle that had taken all she could give. But she had prevailed, she had won.

To address her country, her people, tonight needed to be special. Monica Drew decided to speak to her people directly from the most powerful office in the world, the Oval office.

Although it was an unusual venue, she wanted to address her nation sitting behind Lincoln's desk, a desk at which all important decisions were made.

The room was crowded, cameras, anxious reporters filling the small office. As she approached the desk, sat in the chair, she adjusted one of the many microphones. Monica Drew was dressed all in red, a red pants suit, red the color of power. She hesitated for a moment awaiting the signal that she was on air.

"My fellow" she began as she experienced a coughing spell, one she had many of during the speeches in the last few weeks of the campaign.

"Please excuse me", she said, now coughing more violently. She reached for a Kleenex tissue from the box which had been placed on her desk. She gently wiped her lips and looked at the tissue. It was stained with blood. Blood that had come from her lungs, from the tumor only she and her physician knew about. She ignored it, put the tissue on her desk and tried to continue.

"My fellow Americans," now another coughing spell, more blood. Now all of America watching knew she was in distress, clearly saw the blood saturating her tissue. She had hidden it well, hid it for months, hid it as she had hidden much of her past, her emails, her true medical records, her failures as Secretary of State. Only a few months ago her doctor had told her that she was suffering from a fatal disease, a primary lymphoma of the brain. A tumor fatal within a few months if left untreated. A tumor that rarely spreads beyond the brain and the eyes. But her tumor acted differently, it had spread to her lungs.

She had urged her doctor and the one specialist her doctor had consulted, a renowned neurologist of George Washington University, to keep her ailment a secret. She did not reveal it to anyone, not her husband, not her only child, not to the American people. Afterall, revealing the truth had been one of her strengths. Even as a child, as a student at the Yale law school, as the wife of a President, as a Senator, as a Secretary of State, revealing the truth had been her forte.

She had dismissed her doctor's recommendation to seek treatment. That, she decided, would become public, and prevent her from her ultimate goal, to be the first woman President of the United States.

As she slumped back in the chair, the most powerful chair in the world, she smiled. She knew she would die soon. She did not mind. Not now. She finally had accomplished her dream, to be the first woman President of the United States, the most powerful woman in the world.

Monica Drew was a fighter. She was resilient, she never gave up. Although her cancer had spread to her lungs, she had refused any therapy. Deep down she believed she would win her war with cancer. After all, had she not defeated many of her opponents.

She recovered quickly from the moment in the Oval Office when all of America had watched. It was exhaustion, the White House speaker explained. And America believed it, after all it had been a vigorous campaign.

POTSDAM, SANSSOUCI

The Prince loved Sanssouci, he loved the tranquility, the history, he loved his walks in the beautiful part. Here his mind was free, here he could plan and dream as surely as his forefather Fredrick the Great had done.

But as dearly as Fredrick the Great had a clear understanding of the politics of his time, so has Prince Wilhelm. Perhaps more, Prince Wilhelm thought as he took a short stroll in the beautiful gardens surrounding the palace. Clearly his forefather was a visionary who had made Prussia one of the greatest powers in Europe.

Wilhelm of Hohenzolken knew that the European Union he had built was in trouble. He understood that Britain's exit from the E.U., Brexit, had been orchestrated by the Russians paid for in billions of rubles. And he knew the true cause was nationalism, a desire to close Britain's borders, to once more make Britain what it once had been, a wish by Her Majesty, the Queen of England.

Of course, the immigration issue, the anti-immigrant rhetoric of the U.K.'s Independence Party, calling for Britain to shut its borders, was Buckingham's front. It was the resurgence to nationalism, to make Britain once more what she had been, that was Her Majesty's command.

The Prince was well informed. After all, he thought we all are family. Of course, Brexit could be a threat to his plan of a unified European Union. Yet he had never considered Britain to be a part of the Union.

But now Brexit challenged his plan, his plan to make Europe a world power. It was not Brexit, he welcomed it, it was the threat of other countries leaving the E.U.

Strong movement towards the right by Austria, Sweden, Italy, Denmark, Hungary, France, Netherlands, all concerned him. The Prince needed to unify the E.U., to establish a balance of power in the world. He needed to stop the desire of "galloping populism", to the voices of the far right calling for their once open countries to close up and turn inward.

And he needed to expand the European Union to make it a true world power, to establish the balance he knew the world needed.

As he neared the Marble Room, he reminded himself of his family, how once all had ruled the world, how they were all born from the same stock, the Tsars, the Habsburgs, the Hohenzollern, the "Windsors", the kings of Spain, France and more, all family. Now the Prince realized that the call from Madrid was a gift sent from heaven.

CHAPTER XXII

BERLIN, JAGDSCHLOSS GRUNEWALD

Prince Wilhelm decided that the Jagdschloss Grunewald would be the best place to meet, to meet again some of his relatives, Klaus Wilhelm of Prussia and his son, the Grand Duke of Russia, the undisputed head of the Imperial Family of Russia, educated at Oxford who had worked at the European Parliament in Brussels before forming his own company.

As the Prince walked the grounds of the Schloss in the Grunewald, Berlin's expansive forest, he reminisced. The Jagdschloss, the oldest preserved castle in Berlin, was built in 1542 by Joachim II of Brandenburg as a hunting lodge. It is surrounded by forest and lakes, a secluded place to meet family.

Prince Wilhelm had been firm. No one should know about the meeting between him and his Russian family. No one he had instructed. The Prince knew about the FSB but most importantly they were to have no knowledge of the meeting. Neither was Adam. This was a family meeting. There were to be no interruptions. The Prince had planned the evening in microscopic detail, security was at its highest alert, the Prince wanted no one to know, not to detect who his visitors were.

It was like they had always known each other. They hugged, kissed, it was family.

"Wilhelm", Klaus exclaimed, "do you realize you and I were born on the same date, in the same hospital almost at the same hour?"

"No", Wilhelm responded in disbelief, "on October 14?"

"Yes," Klaus responded, clapping his hands.

"Father, please let's get to why we have come here," Klaus' son the Grand Duke of Russia, the head of the Imperial Family of Russia, urged on. "You know I love Wilhelm, I respect what he has done for Europe, to unite it, to make it a world power. But now with Brexit, Britain leaving the E.U., I want to know his perspective. He told us at our last meeting he wants Russia to become a member. I want to know all the details, I want to help, want to participate, want to know what he thinks should happen next?"

"I agree, son," Klaus responded, "that's why we came here. Wilhelm, my son adores you. He is a staunch supporter of the European Union."

"OK," Wilhelm responded, "before dinner or after?"

All three of the royals were sitting in the library of the hunting lodge, a fire blazing in the rustic fireplace.

"Now," the young, impatient heir to the Russian throne continued, "I have followed your politics closely, you are the best."

"Thank you," Prince Wilhelm responded, "but before I continue, let's all have an aperitif."

"Agreed," Klaus answered.

All asked for a glass of champagne.

"OK, Uncle. May I call you that? I have no idea how we are related. Our families are so screwed up. But I would like to call you uncle, if you don't mind?"

"I would love it, it would touch my heart, please call me uncle." Prince Wilhelm replied.

The fire in the 500-year-old fireplace was fully ablaze. All lights in the lodge had been turned off. Only the fire lit the room. All of the princes were sitting on a large leather couch facing the burning fire.

"Uncle", the young Grand Duke from Madrid, asked, "you created the E.U., but now there is Brexit, and I know for the EU to survive we need Russia."

Prince Wilhelm liked the young man from Madrid, the Grand Duke, the head of Russia's royal family, a descendant of his family, the Hohenzollerns.

"It is a bit complex. But I will try to explain it. The E.U. you know was not really my brain child, but I made it happen. Europe can only survive if it unites. Unfortunately, we let Britain enter the Union. They always are a pain in the ass. Always want special consideration. They were never true partners, never had their hearts in it. You know they really are not Europeans, always asking for special treatment, and no Euro."

"So, what does Brexit mean?" the Grand Duke interrupted.

"A dream come true," Prince Wilhelm responded. "I never wanted Britain in the E.U. but my friend the French P.M. urged me otherwise. It was always a mistake. But now let's talk about the big picture. Now Britain wants to get back into the E.U., I oppose it. They are a pain in the ass. But more importantly Russia also opposes it. Russia intends to destroy the E.U., it would make Russia more powerful. Mr. Pavlov has spent millions of dollars bribing British politicians to vote for Brexit. And then he called for a Euro exit, he wants all countries to leave the E.U. A weak E.U., or no E.U., he thinks means a strong Russia."

"I am with you," the Grand Duke of Russia, answered, "but how do we stop him?"

"Well, as you know, there has been a dramatic shift to the right in European politics. There has been a resurgence of nationalism across the E.U. Fragmented nationalism, nationalism only on behalf of your own country. It will weaken the Union, perhaps your own country. But if we define nationalism in terms of Europe, a European Union, nationalism will become very powerful."

"Uncle," the grand Duke asked, "how do we do that?"

"Simple," Prince Wilhelm replied, "nationalism by definition is a shared group feeling in the significance of a geographic and sometimes demographic region seeking independence for its culture or ethnicity that holds that group together. Clearly our families, the Romanovs, the Hohenzollerns, the Habsburgs, share that feeling."

Now Klaus Wilhelm of Prussia, the father of the Grand Duke, stood up. He slowly walked towards the fireplace, then turned and faced Prince Wilhelm.

"I like it all, you are suggesting that all the European royal families should unite, create a strong European Union. I agree. Clearly Germany is ready to do so, as is Austria, since last month the newly elected chancellor also is one of us, another member of the Royal House of Europe. But Russia is a problem. Do you have a solution?"

"I do", Prince Wilhelm responded as he lit another one of his favorite cigars, a Padron, a torpedo, a special edition.

Prince Wilhelm leaned back in his leather couch, put his arm around the young Duke of Russia, the claimant to the Imperial House of Russia. Now he knew he was in control. Now he knew Europe, perhaps the world, would once again be ruled by the rightful people, the Royal Families of Europe.

CHAPTER XXIII

VIENNA, BALLHAUSPLATZ 2

The office of the Austrian chancellery in the Inner Stadt of Vienna located on the edge of the grounds of Hofburg Imperial Palace, only a few minutes' walk from the Austrian Parliament building. The Palace built in the 13th century, now is the official residence of the President of Austria, the ceremonial figurehead of the government.

Werner von Habsburg, the newly elected chancellor of Austria, stood alone in the office of the Austrian chancellery in Vienna. Werner is the current head of the house of the Habsburg-Lorraine dynasty since his father Olaf died a few years ago. Werner is a staunch supporter of the European Union, had served as a member of European Parliament and was an advocate for the Pan European movement, the oldest European unification movement which had its roots in the publishing of Count Richar Nikolaus von Coudenhove-Kalergi's manifesto "Paneuropa" in 1923.

Werner's father had become its International President in 1973. Notable members include Albert Einstein, Thomas Mann, Konrad Adenauer, Sigmund Freud, and others. Even Winston Churchill lauded the movement's work for a unified Europe in a Zurich speech in 1946. How ironic Werner thought now Britain had voted to leave the union.

Shortly after the vote, perhaps two or three weeks had gone by, Werner had received a telephone call from Berlin. It had been Germany's chancellor himself calling to congratulate him on his election as chancellor of Austria. But Prince Wilhelm, Germany's Chancellor, then asked Werner for a meeting, a meeting he had said on a topic that lies close to our hearts, the hearts of our families. And then he suggested the meeting place, Habsburg Castle. Werner was surprised, almost in disbelief. Habsburg Castle was the original seat of his house, the House of Habsburg. But now it was a medieval castle, most of it in ruins, located in Habsburg, Switzerland, near the Oar River.

"Habsburg Castle?" he asked, "Why?"

"I know part of the place is in ruins, but the towers are still in great shape. Most importantly, no one will ever know we met there. Secondly, I want us to go back in history, I want to make peace with the Habsburgs and I want it done on your turf."

"Wilhelm, I know, peace with my family is not on top of your agenda. Tell me your true reason, why do we need to meet?"

"You are right, Werner," the Prince responded, always knowing Werner was not going to buy his line of peace, but Wilhelm wanted Werner to take the initiative.

"It's about the European Union, about Brexit. I know how strongly you believe in the E.U., as much as I do."

"Yes," Werner answered, "Brexit worries me, it could destroy all my father and I have wanted to accomplish, a unified Europe."

"On the contrary," Prince Wilhelm replied, "Brexit is exactly the answer to a unified Europe. I can't discuss it on the telephone, please let's meet, let's meet at the Habsburg Castle three days from now. My people will make all the arrangements. Great talking to you and "Auf wiedersehen". A click, Berlin and Vienna were no longer connected.

Werner von Habsburg, the newly elected chancellor of Austria, the direct descendant of the throne of Austria, placed the receiver back on his phone. Werner loved old things and he loved his phone, a phone with a dial, a phone more than 30 years old.

Werner leaned back in his chair behind his mahogany desk, he rubbed his eyes, he needed to think. Clearly, he thought, the E.U. was in trouble, all the talk about Brexit, Grexit, and more countries leaving the union, was not what he wanted, not what his father Olaf had worked so hard for. And he also knew that the Chancellor of Germany, Prince Wilhelm of Hohenzollern was a brilliant politician. Werner could not wait to meet with him at Habsburg Castle.

CHAPTER XXIV

CAPRI, ITALY

The sea of the bay of Naples was as blue and calm as Adam had ever remembered it. There was not a cloud in the sky. The gozzo, Victorino's gozzo, was drifting aimlessly a few hundred yards off the rocky shore of the island of Capri. Adam had asked his friend Victorino, the captain of the gozzo to turn off the motor and just let the wooden boat drifts.

Adam was alone, Nicole had decided to take the train to Milan to shop. Adam had quickly agreed, he loved being the only passenger on Victorino's gozzo, to lie alone on the large launchpad in the bow of the boat, to relax and to think. No one to disturb him.

Today he was not drinking his usual favorite Pinot Grigio, today he was drinking Cristal Champagne. Today was a special occasion. Today he had been paid by three different governments for the same job. Adam stood up and reached for his white linen shirt, he did not unbutton it but merely slipped it over his head. He had had enough sun, already he could see the burn on his muscular body. Slowly he walked back to the aft of the gozzo, retrieved one of the several Cristal Champagne bottles he had bought for the occasion, opened one and poured first a glass for Victorino and then a glass for himself.

"Salute," he said to the captain of the boat.

"Salute," Victorino replied.

Adam turned to walk back to the sun pad on the bow of the boat. As he did he reached for the small cigar case he had left on the Captain's chair in the cockpit of the gozzo. He took out one of the cigars, cut the end of it and lit it. Adam did not smoke often, but when he did he always smoked his favorite cigar, a Padron torpedo. With a Cristal champagne glass in his left hand, a Padron in his right, he returned to the sun pad at the bow of the gozzo. He did not sit down. Instead, he looked at the sea, noticed the beauty of the color of the water, but more importantly noticed the calmness, the stillness, the peace of the sea. This week he had accomplished all. Three governments had paid him handsomely for an assassination, and he never had to pull the trigger. Millions of dollars had been transferred into his bank accounts, more money than he could ever spend.

He took a draw from his favorite cigar, he did not inhale, he never did. He just liked the taste of it. As he let the smoke leave his mouth, he made a decision. Adam always liked to make his decisions when he was alone, relaxed, under no pressure. Adam decided to leave the assassination business, Adam decided to retire.

"Victorino," he said, "please take me back to marina piccola, I have news for Nicole, news I know she will love to hear."

Adam rushed into his luxurious apartment on the island of Capri. But there was no Nicole, only two messages on the telephone. The first was from Nicole, "Honey, I will be late, I found the greatest clothes, no not really clothes, but shoes, can't wait to show you. Love you."

The second message was more somber, it was direct clear-cut, it was German.

"Adam," Prince Wilhelm said, "there is a meeting, a very important one. I need you to be there, it is a must. It will take place four days from now; the place is the Ocean Club in the Bahamas. All arrangements for you have been made. Just show up and you must!"

Adam walked away from his answering machine and entered his shower. He needed to relax, needed the hot water soothing his tense body, and he needed his lover Nicole.

He had barely stepped out of the shower, his body still wet, when Nicole rushed to him, embraced him, kissed him on the mouth.

"Adam, Adam," she exclaimed, "there is no way you can imagine what I bought, the best dresses, the best shoes, let me show you."

"I expected you much later, what happened?" Adam asked. But Adam had little interest in Nicole's purchases, he wanted to see none of them. But he wanted Nicole.

He went towards her, picked her up and carried her into their bedroom.

Adam had already finished his customary run around the island of Capri and the aroma of the fresh coffee awoke Nicole.

Adam was busy preparing Nicole's favorite breakfast, two eggs over light, bacon and toast, also a glass of orange juice, freshly squeezed.

Nicole and Adam always enjoyed their breakfast on their large terrace overlooking the bay of Naples, and the rock of Faglioni.

"Nicole," Adam began, "last week was unreal, everyone paid us so much money, now we can retire, never ever worry."

"Let's do it," Nicole responded enthusiastically, "where is the Champagne?"

"Sorry, I forgot it."

He rushed back into the apartment, retrieved a bottle of Cristal Champagne and two glasses.

"Here, I am sorry, but I celebrated by myself while you were in Milan shopping."

"By yourself?" Nicole asked.

"Yes, I asked Victorino to take me out on his gozzo. I wanted to celebrate, and I wanted to make a decision. I needed to be alone."

"What did you decide ?" Nicole asked.

"Well," Adam responded, now uneasy, "I had thought about giving it all up, about retiring."

"What a wonderful idea," Nicole exclaimed as she hugged Adam and kissed him on the mouth.

"I love it, no more guns, no more intrigue, just you and me loving each other."

"Yeah, that's sort of what I had in mind," Adam answered.

"What do you mean, had in mind, I don't understand?" Nicole asked as she looked Adam straight in the eye.

"Well today I received a phone call, things changed a bit, made me rethink the retirement idea."

"What do you mean, what things?" Nicole was almost angrily demanding.

"Prince Wilhelm called me, asked me and you to attend a meeting. It was not an option, it was a must."

"What kind of meeting ?" Nicole asked.

"It is all about the European Union, all the players will be there. It is at The Ocean Club," Adam responded.

"O.K," Nicole answered, "Let's go. I love The Ocean Club."

CHAPTER XXV

PARADISE ISLAND, BAHAMAS

Prince Wilhelm had rented all the villas at the Ocean Club. Not really he, once again it was a wealthy German industrialist, a close friend of the Prince.

Once again they did not meet in one of the meeting rooms at the fashionable Hotel. Instead they met again on the beach. A small tent had been erected there, it contained a small table and several chairs.

All were in attendance. All the people Prince Wilhelm had asked to be there, the new chancellor of Austria, the Grand Duke of Russia, and his father, and, of course, Adam and Nicole.

"Clearly, if Russia becomes part of the E.U.," Prince Wilhelm began as all had been served Cristal Champagne, "there will be no Eurexit, then there will be a true balance of power in the world.".

"We have discussed this at our last meeting, we all agree, but do we get Russia to join, how do we eliminate Mr. Pavlov?" the Grand Duke asked anxiously.

"Now that is the key," Prince Wilhelm answered. "Now you need to trust my judgment. Only weeks ago, you may recall, there was another person who presented an obstacle. I took care of it."

All were silent. All knew he was referring to the Chief of MI6.

"Russia loves a strong leader, does not mind an authoritative government, or even dictatorship. In case of Mr. Pavlov's death the void of strong, authoritative leadership has to be filled immediately. The Russian people, I am certain, will elect a Royal, they will call for the Grand Duke to lead their country. They will do so because the Russian people want to be part of the EU, be part of Europe."

"Uncle", the Grand Duke replied enthusiastically as he carefully listened. "It could work."

"Father," he said as he turned to Prince Klaus Wilhelm of Prussia, "what do you think?"

"I want to know what Baron von Rosenberg has to say, Israel is important to us, we need their support.,"Wilhelm continued.

"I will assure you that my country will do all to help this cause. But the devil lies in details. How do we eliminate the President of the Russian Federation?" Israel's Prime Minister asked.

"That is why I have invited Adam," Prince Wilhelm answered, as he gestured towards Adam who was standing at the opening of the tent.

"Adam is the best at that sort of business. Let's hear what he has planned."

Adam entered the open tent and faced all the Royals.

"At the moment I have not formulated a detailed plan. But I know it can be done. I needed to be certain that all of you agree with Prince Wilhelm. Now I know. I can't do it alone, particularly I need the help of the Mossad, your intelligence service, Mr. Prime Minister," Adam said as he looked at the Baron. "The head of your agency, Maza, is a good friend of mine, he trained me. One thing is clear, there can be no trace pointing to any of you, all fingers have to be pointed to the C.I.A."

"How can you accomplish that?" Israel's Prime Minister asked.

"The first step is that you inform Maza, let me meet with him, we'll figure it out."

"O.K." the Grand Duke of Russia chimed in. "But will you give us all the details of the plan, where, when, how?"

"Of course," Adam replied, "I won't lift a finger without your approval."

Prince Wilhelm turned to the head agent of the BND, "Please, serve us the best Russian Vodka, we need to celebrate."

CHAPTER XXVI

CAPRI, ITALY

Adam Bergman and Maza Sharef met only three days after the meeting of the Royals at the "Ocean Club". Both were clad in short bathing suits lounging on the sun pad of Victorino's gozzo. Adam had chosen the gozzo, no listening devices, no one following them, both alone in the bay of Naples. Adam also had not asked Nicole to join them. He wanted to be alone with Maza, the head of Israel's Mossad. This mission was the most important one of his life and Adam trusted no one, the reason he believed he was still alive.

"Maza, what do you think?" Adam asked as he passed a glass of Pinot Grigio to his friend.

"Well. First of all, you never make it easy."

"Easy," Adam replied with a smile, "it is never easy, that is why we are being paid the big bucks."

"I know you are," Maza replied with a grin, "but I am only a government employee, get the same salary no matter how tough the job is."

"Perhaps you should change your employer, come and work with me." Adam said fully knowing Maza would never accept.

"Adam, you and I are very much alike, but also very different. We are the best at our business but you do it for money and for the challenge. I do it for my country."

"I accept that, we all have our reasons," Adam said as he poured himself another glass of wine. Maza had barely touched his glass.

"To get to Mr. Pavlov is almost impossible, he is too well protected."

"Come on," Adam interjected, "are you telling me Mr. Kennedy, the President of the USA, was not well protected."

"Of course, you are right, it can be done." Maza said knowing Adam had already formulated a plan.

"Adam," he continued," I know you have thought about this, have an idea of how to do it."

"You are right." Adam said as he rose from the large sun pad in the bow of the gozzo and stretched himself. "I have thought about it day and night since I left the meeting with all the Royals. The key is that it has to be the American, the CIA, who kills him. And we need to find a place where he is most vulnerable."

"Where is that?" Maza asked, fully knowing the answer.

"Clearly not in Moscow, but in Sochi where he loves to go and relax. But how do we get close to him there?" Maza continued.

"He loves to ride a horse on the beach there, I thought about frogmen, a drone strike, but none will work. The FSB is one of the best. But I also know you have infiltrated the FSB, have agents there."

"True," Maza responded, "but only two."

"Well," Adam continued, "we only need one. Does Mr. Pavlov ride the same horse on the beach at Sochi?"

"No," Maza replied, "he has three, but he favors one, Chloe."

"No problem," Adam continued, "We will place a bomb in the horses. All three of them."

"A bomb in the horses?" Maza now was curious, "how do we do that?"

"Well, one of your agents will do it, place bombs under the skin of the horses. A vet can teach him how to do it, and it should be done before Mr. Pavlov goes to Sochi. Can you do it?"

"Of course," Maza replied with a smile, "as you said nothing in our business is impossible. But kill a horse?"

"A small price to pay to save Europe," Adam said. "And your agent will use his cell phone to trigger the bomb."

"I kind of like the idea," Maza said as he asked Adam to fill his glass with Pinot Grigio. Maza liked the wine Adam had chosen.

"But how do we link the kill to the CIA?" Maza wanted to know.

"Frankly, I don't care for the link to the CIA, but the Royals want it. Obviously a bomb will immediately point the finger to the terrorists groups, but we will use an explosive commonly used by the Americans. Then let the Russians guess who committed the assassination."

"Adam, I like your plan, it could work. Now I know why they pay you the big bucks."

Both hugged each other. Both were certain their plan could work. Adam walked back toward the stern of the boat and asked Victorino, the captain of the gozzo, to take them back to Marina Piccola, the small marina on the isle of Capri.

CHAPTER XXVII

BERLIN, GERMANY

It was late. He stood by the large window of his office in the Chancellery and watched the sunset over the Tiergarten, the large park which once had been the hunting grounds of his forefathers. He had wanted to go home early, sit on the boat dock of his home on Lake Wannsee, and smoke a cigar. Then he wanted his favorite meal, a Wiener Schnitzel, prepared by his wife. He had eaten Wiener Schnitzel all over Europe, but no one made it better than his wife. It was not to be. All day he had struggled with the problem his predecessor had left him, the problem of immigrants entering his country. Four years ago, when he was elected Chancellor of Germany, he had campaigned on the platform to keep immigrants out of the country. Clearly then it is what his people wanted. But Prince Wilhelm was a student of history. He remembered his forefather's tolerance to immigrants, allowing thousands of refugees from Austria to settle in Prussia after they had been evicted from Salzburg, Austria. It was those immigrants that had been a factor in Prussia's rise to power.

Yet he was not sure. He had campaigned against the open door policy of his predecessor and he had won by a landslide. Clearly his countrymen opposed the influx of immigrants, but deep in his heart he was not sure. Then his telephone rang, it was the secure line only few people had access to. Quickly he walked towards his large mahogany desk, and picked up the phone.

"Prince," the voice familiar to Prince Wilhelm said, "I have a plan."

"OK, Adam, let's meet, tell me all about it."

"Where, when?" Adam asked.

"Adam, there is this park in Dahlem, a suburb of Berlin, called "Thielpark."

"Of course," Adam replied, "I grew up there, know the place like the back of my hand."

"There is a very large stone there, a large rock actually, called the "Findling", from the stone ages, do you know it?"

"Are you kidding, of course I do, always tried to climb it, never did until I was a teenager. Then I jumped onto it from the stone wall next to it, a game we always played when I grew up there."

"Excellent, let's meet there the day after tomorrow at 1 p.m. Does that work for you?"

"Perfect," Adam replied, "The Findling."

Adam had not been back for years to where he had grown up, attended his grammar school, Lanz Schule, to the park, Thielpark, where he and his friends had played cowboys and Indians. It also was where he first kissed a girl on one of the many park benches in the park.

Adam took a private jet to the Berlin Brandenburg Airport. He had not asked Nicole to accompany him, no need he had told her, just a meeting with a banker.

Adam did not take a taxi from the airport to the Thielplatz, the U-Bahn station near his meeting spot with the Prince. He took the subway. He left the subway at Hohenzollern Platz and took the bus

100, the bus he had taken many times, many years ago. He knew it would stop at the Thielplatz. Adam was early, 30 minutes early. He decided to stroll across the street and head towards the church he had attended as a child. First he walked through the small park adjacent to the church, he glanced at the small pond on which he had played ice hockey in the winter. It had been much larger than, almost a lake, he mused. Suddenly he turned, making sure he was not being followed.

Then he walked back to the station of the U3 subway line, the Thielplatz Bahnhof. There at the kiosk he bought an ice cream cone, a purchase he had done often many years ago when he was but a child.

He had looked down Bruemmerstrasse and Loehleinstrasse, the street he had lived on as a child. Both ran parallel to the subway, both were empty. No one was following.

Adam entered the "Thielpark" and slowly strolled along the walkway to the right of the small hill which in the winter time had been one of his favorite sledding hills. Often he had steered his "Flexible Flyer," a gift from his grandmother, down the slope. He knew even today it was a favorite winter spot for many of the local Berlilners.

Adam knew that the "Findling", the Thielstein, a remnant of the ice age, was only a short distance from the entrance of the park. It was located in a small recess to the right of the path. As a child Adam had come here often, it was the meeting place for him and his friends. Here they all would come and play their favorite game, cowboys and Indians. Adam did not recall how the choice was made, but he did remember that he always wanted to be a cowboy.

As Adam turned off the path and entered the small, intimate cove of the park, he saw him. Prince Wilhelm was sitting on top of the large rock, the Findling. The Prince had a broad smile on his face and waved Adam to join him. Unlike many years ago, Adam easily climbed the "Thielstein" and sat down next to the Prince.

"Adam", the Prince said as he hugged his friend, "I wanted to meet you here, meet you at your favorite spot."

"How did you know?" Adam asked genuinely surprised.

"Well," the Prince replied, smiling even more broadly, "that's why we employ spies, and you, more than any other person I know, should know."

"I do," Adam replied, "but you still surprised me."

Adam did not see any of the Prince's secret service agents, but he knew they were here.

"All right," Prince Wilhelm continued, "although I like your favorite spot, the rock is hard and not comfortable to sit on."

Then Adam explained his plan to assassinate the President of the Russian Federation, the plan he had designed, the plan his friend, the head of the Mossad, had agreed upon.

"Adam," the Prince responded after having carefully listened to Adam's strategy. "I love it, you are a genius. Now I need to inform all the other members, the Grand Duke, Karl and the Prime Minister of Israel. I think they all will agree."

Now Prince Wilhelm stood up, his feet firmly planted on the large rock, "how will I know it is a go?" Adam asked.

"Simple," the Prince replied. "Three days from now I will ask Victorino to take you out on his gozzo. While on the boat asked him for a glass of your favorite Pinot Grigio, and if he serves you a Veltiner, my favorite, you know it is a go."

The Prince nodded and headed towards one of the black limousines parked in the street," Im Schwarzen Grund", just outside of the park. Adam turned to see his friend leave. Then he saw them all, he knew they had been there. Six BND agents, Prince Wilhelm's security agents. They quickly rushed the Prince into two of the armor plated Mercedes cars waiting, motors running. As the vehicles drove away Adam wondered about the Russian FSB agents Mr. Pavlov had sent to protect the Prince. Where were they, he wondered. the Prince evaded them? He did not know.

CHAPTER XXVIII

THE WHITE HOUSE, WASHINGTON, D.C

Monica Drew sat in the Oval Office, she was concerned. Since her last meeting with her Chief of Staff she decided she did not like the man. Instead she decided to consult her husband. She also had become more informed about the effect of Brexit. Her husband was well informed, he had urged her not to ignore what was happening in Europe. Brexit he had told her, will have more of an impact on America than just on the economy. Brexit could change the balance of power in the world. Her husband, a former President of the United States, knew how to play the game. Monica did not. When she was elected President of the United States she decided it was payback time. Now she had to let her husband know that she was the alpha dog, no longer playing second fiddle, no longer tolerating all his affairs with younger women. And she knew how to emasculate him, to take him out of the limelight he loved so much. For months during her campaign she had never listened to his advice, on the contrary, she often took the opposite opinion. To her it did not matter that it may be bad for America, it was good for her. And what was good for her was all that mattered.

It was a conversation with her daughter that changed her mind, that told her to forget the past, to bury the ax, to become the leader America had elected. Monica Drew had struggled with that idea for weeks. How could she ever forgive the man who lied to her, the man who was deceitful. That's when her daughter had reminded her that she was no different than her husband. Remember, she had said, what you did and said about Benghazi, about your emails, about our foundation. Are you really different from Dad, she had asked.

That's when Monica Drew looked deep into her soul. No, she decided, I am no different. I seek power, money, no matter the means, no matter the cost. And she knew there was no one better than her husband to accomplish it all. From now on she would pay attention to his advice, and his advice had been to work more closely with her Chief of Staff, Roger Kiefer.

"Roger," she said as her Chief of Staff was sitting in her Oval Office. "There is more to Brexit than you have told me."

"I tried," Roger responded, but you had decided not to listen."

"OK" Monica replied impatiently, "let bygones be bygones. Now I want to learn the whole picture."

"Madame President," Roger said more confidently, sensing that the President of the USA was now willing to listen to his advice. "The effect of Brexit will not only have a major impact on our economy, it could change the balance of power in the world."

"How is that?" Monica Drew asked.

"The Russian President is determined to destroy the E.U.. If he is successful Russia again will be a world power, a power greater than the USA."

"Greater than the USA?" Monica Drew asked in disbelief.

"Yes", her Chief of Staff responded. "He will control all of Europe."

"We can not let that happen. Not on my watch. How can we stop it?"

"Right now we are behind the eight ball. We missed our opportunities, hesitated, and did not make the right decisions."

"Please, Roger. Don't dwell on the past. What can we do now to change it?"

"There may be a way. Our intelligence tells us that there is a plot by members of the European Union to stop Mr. Pavlov, the President of the Russian Federation."

"Stop him? What do you mean?" Monica Drew was anxious to know.

"We have information, I am not sure of its veracity, that there is a plot to kill the President of the Russian Federation."

"Kill him?" Monica asked in disbelief. "Then what?"

"Well, from what I know, from what our intelligence believes, the E.U. is planning it. But I am not sure."

"If getting rid of Mr. Pavlov is the answer to maintain our position as the leader in the world, do all you can do to help them."

"Help them?" the Chief of Staff asked.

"Yes," the President of the United States replied.

"Help them to kill the bastard. Am I clear?"

As clear, as transparent, as your emails, her Chief of Staff thought, as he left the Oval Office.

CHAPTER XXIX

BUCKINGHAM PALACE, LONDON

The Queen of England had asked for a meeting with her Prime Minister, Margaret Sawyer. The Queen was now concerned about Brexit, a policy she had initiated, a policy she believed was in the best interest of her kingdom. But now she had second thoughts, no one had ever explained to her the potential economic impact on her country, the possibility of Russia destroying the E.U. and becoming Europe's leader. All the Queen had wanted was England to be once more a major power, a dynasty, a world power, the status England deserved.

"Your Highness," Margaret Sawyer began after both had been served tea in a reception room of Buckingham Palace, "Your Highness, your decision to leave the European Union was a mistake."

"My decision?" the Queen of England asked, somewhat disturbed. "You recommended it, supported it."

"Your Royal Highness, may I be frank?"

"Of course," the Queen responded.

"The two of us had different agendas," the Prime Minister continued, "I only wanted to get elected. I had put my faith in the fact that all British people would follow your wish, your wish to exit the E. U. to make Britain once more the power she had once been. And I was right, I was elected to the office of Prime Minister, but I also always knew to leave the E.U. would destroy Britain."

"Are you telling me that you supported an idea, an idea you knew was not in the best interest of our country?" The Queen was irritated.

"Yes, your Highness. Number one rule in our country is to never disagree with the Royal House. A rule I am sure you are well aware of, a rule that your family has insisted upon for centuries. Number two rule for a politician is you advocate what the people want. It never matters whether it is right, wrong, good or bad, for the country. You go with the flow, that's how you get elected."

The Queen of England swiveled in her leather chair, to be lectured today by a Commoner was not on her royal agenda. But she composed herself, did not speak for several minutes. Then she continued.

"Well," she said, looking down her nose, almost defiantly, "well what do you propose we do about it all?"

"Your Highness, "the Prime Minister responded, "Your Excellency," and she exaggerated the words, "we need to reenter the European Union."

"My God," the Queen immediately exclaimed, "re enter the E.U.? My people voted against it, England clearly wants to stand on its own feet."

"Your Highness," the Prime Minister responded, somberly, "England has no feet without the E. U., we will go bankrupt, we will become a third world country."

The Queen was shocked. It had been her dream to once more make her country what it once had been, a world power, a leader, an empire. But these dreams were only dreams living within the walls of Buckingham Palace. And now the Queen of England finally realized it.

"Please," she now asked more humbly as she addressed her Prime Minister, "please, how do we handle it?"

"The answer is easy, we need to get back into the E.U. The way to do it is our problem."

"How is that?" the Queen asked.

"The E.U. does no longer want Britain to be part of it. As a matter of fact, Prince Wilhelm of Hohenzollern, a relative of yours, I believe, is vehemently against it."

"Why?" the Queen asked, knowing well the animosity within her family.

"Perhaps you should call him, ask him that question." The Prime Minister now on her turf, challenged. The Queen was clearly agitated now, she was not used to having Commoners question her, not even her own Prime Minister.

"All right," she said. "Maybe I will. But tell me the whole picture, I need to know all of it."

Now the Prime Minister knew she had succeeded. Now she would be able to convince the Queen to take the right route, her route.

"It really is quite simple," the Prime Minister continued. "Brexit was only the first step in Russia's plan to destroy the European Union. We were the first pawn in Mr. Pavlov's game of chess. And he won. He wanted us to leave the E.U., he wants all of the E.U. members to leave, a Eurexit. A weak E.U. means a strong Russia."

"All right," the Queen interrupted, "I see the picture. How can we help?"

"Simple," the Prime Minister responded, "forget about your dreams of a revived British Empire, get into survival mode, do all you can to get us back into the E.U."

"How can I do that?" the Queen asked.

"Well, call your family, call the relatives you always thought were not worthy. Now they are."

CHAPTER XXX

CAPRI, ITALY

Adam and Maza had decided to give the assassination attempt of the President of Russia, the code name "Secretariat" and the jockey, the assassin, "Wild Bill".

Three horses Adam thought as he relaxed on the sun pad of Victorino's gozzo. Adam loved horses, but he knew it was the only way. To place a small explosive device under a horse's skin was a procedure double agents could easily perform, Maza had assured Adam.

Maza's two agents who were working undercover in the FSB were two of his best. Both had been born in Russia, had grown up there, were university educated and had been recruited by the FSB, Russia's intelligence agency. Unbeknown to the FSB both men had distant Jewish roots, both had a Jewish grandmother who had secretly taught them all about the Jewish faith.

Maza decided to only use one of his agents, his "Wild Bill" for "Secretariat." In case the plot failed he did not want to lose all the assets he had within the FSB. When Maza had suggested to Adam to only have one Wild Bill, Adam felt uncomfortable. He knew how important this mission was, a mission that would change the balance of power, a mission that could change the world.

Adam and Victorino were alone on the gozzo, the boat was hardly moving. There was no music, neither man spoke, there was only the sound of the gentle waves meeting the hull of the wooden boat. Victorino knew Adam well, years ago they had become friends, Victorino knew when Adam wanted silence.

No, Adam thought as he rolled over onto his back on the large sun pad at the bow of Victorino's boat, no, no way. I am not sitting hundreds of miles away when the most important trigger will be pulled. An assassination more important than the one of JFK. It is my mission, my trigger and I will pull it, he decided. After all, I am the best.

As soon as Victorino dropped Adam off at the Marina Piccola, Adam headed for the small public telephone booth adjacent to the Marina. He used one of his cell phones, one he would toss into the bay of Naples after the call to contact Maza, the head of the Mossad.

The phone in Tel Aviv, at the Dafora building, Mossad's headquarters,only rang twice, then Maza answered.

"What's up?" he asked, knowing it was Adam calling.

"I changed my mind about Secretariat, I need to be Wild Bill. I need your help. Need you to get me in the saddle."

"OK" Maza responded, "but the jockey I have is excellent, he can win."

"I know," Adam replied, "but it is my race."

"Understood," was the voice from Tel Aviv, the call was over.

Maza was in disbelief. Adam had designed the perfect plan to kill the President of the Russian Federation, and Maza had the man in place who could pull it off. Adam could just sit back in Capri, relax, watch it happen and collect all the money.

But Maza knew. It was not the money that motivated Adam, it never was. It was the challenge, and the challenge meant he had to be there, he had to pull the trigger. Maza understood.

Nicole did not, not at once. After Adam had called Maza, he slowly walked up the steep incline from Marina Piccola to his apartment. He walked slowly because he needed to think about an explanation, convince Nicole that he had to go to Sochi, he had to kill Vladimir Pavlov.

When he entered his apartment Nicole rushed towards him, put her arms around his neck, and gave him a passionate kiss on the mouth.

Adam was taken aback.

"What's the occasion?" he asked as he noticed the elaborate dinner table which had been set up on his terrace.

"You don't remember?" Nicole asked, her arms still embracing his neck.

"It's our third anniversary, it was three years ago when we first met on the beach in Miami."

"Of course," Adam now recalled. "How can I forget, we were jogging on the beach."

"Let's sit down and have dinner, one of your favorite dishes, scaloppine vitello al limone, mashed potatoes, peas and carrots, and a bottle of Pinot Grigio."

"Nicole," Adam responded, "you think of everything."

Tonight there was a full moon shining its light on the bay of Naples. The sea was calm, but a soft ocean breeze freshened the air. Adam was troubled. Nicole had arranged for a beautiful evening, reminiscing when they first had met, clearly very romantic moments. Yet, Adam's mind was preoccupied with his decision to go to Russia and kill the President of the Russian Federation. He felt like his mind was on a scale, romance on one side, killing the other. Adam managed to balance the scale throughout their wonderful dinner.

It was only when Nicole served him a grappa after dinner that the scale tipped. It tipped toward killing.

"Nicole," Adam said, "I made a decision today, one I need to share with you."

Nicole also had poured herself a grappa, and with the glass in hand sat next to Adam on the large sofa facing the sea.

"OK," she said, "I am all ears." She raised her glass, touched his, and they both tasted the grappa.

"Excellent," Adam exclaimed, "you always buy the best grappa."

"Adam, I want to hear about the decision you made today. I knew there was something troubling you when you came home. Please tell me."

"Nicole, you know who I am. I am a trained assassin, a trained killer, that is not only my profession, but that is me. I have told you about "Secretariat", and today I made the decision to be "Wild Bill.""

"Why?" Nicole asked gently, gently because deep down she knew the reason, always had.

"Secretariat, it is my idea, my race and I need to be the jockey."

"Adam, there is no need for you to win another race, you have won many, all of them. You have more money than we could ever spend. Why one more assignment?" Nicole asked, fully knowing the answer.

"It is not the prize money, Nicole, it is the challenge."

CHAPTER XXXI

Maza Sharef, the Chief of the Mossad, sat in his office in the Dafna building, the headquarters of Israel's renowned intelligence agency. He knew why Adam Bergman wanted to be Wild Bill, pull the trigger. Of course, he thought it was complicated, perhaps impossible, although he had admired Adam's plan to place bombs in the horses. And to some degree, he had thought his two people within the FSB had at least a remote chance to pull it off.

But now Adam insisted on being the assassin. Maza completely understood why Adam wanted to do it, his job, his idea and the ultimate assassination, the ultimate challenge. Maza had asked his staff to research, to explore any way a foreigner could get close to the Russian President. No result, and his agency was the best.

Maza picked up the telephone and called Adam.

"Adam, we have looked at this every possible way. To get you into Russia, a former NSA and Mossad agent, an assassin, there is no way. Let's go back to plan A, have my guy do the job."

"No," Adam responded, "let's wait, just a few more days. We may end up using your cowboy, but I have a hunch, something I noticed at Berlin's Tegel airport in a Mercedes limousine."

LONDON, BUCKINGHAM PALACE

The Queen of England was upset. Her Prime Minister had been very direct, almost not showing the kind of respect the members of her family deserved. After all, they were the rulers of England and Great Britain.

The Prime Minister had painted a bleak picture for the future of her empire, had explained in excruciating detail that the Royal House's decision to leave the European Union was a grave mistake. She had explained to her Royal Highness that the glory of a British empire dream was part of the past. She had said Britain was being treated as a has been by the European Union, and Britain had to get off the high horse, needed to understand that playing second fiddle to France and Germany really was not all that bad. At least it meant survival.

Call my family in Germany? The Queen thought, no way, but maybe my son should do it, she considered. The phone call was brief. The Queen had convinced her son, the Prince of Wales, to make the call.

Wilhelm took the call in his office at the chancellery in Berlin, never would he refuse a call from a Royal, not even a British Royal.

"Wilhelm, this is Prince Albert," the voice began. Already Prince Wilhelm was annoyed, remembering British arrogance, the caller called him Wilhelm, no title, but identified himself with his title, Prince.

It was now that Prince Wilhelm needed to decide how to convey the message, the message that Britain would never ever be allowed to enter the E.U. again. Not while he was alive, their President. He decided to do it the British way,

"Glad to hear from you, how can I help?" Prince Wilhelm responded.

"As you know our people voted to leave the E.U. We now realize it was a mistake. Great Britain, when it rejoins the E.U., will be its greatest asset. It is only when Great Britain is part of the E.U. that the union will survive and thrive. Europe needs Britain, a Europe without Britain, will be a weak Europe."

Prince Wilhelm was in disbelief, the arrogance, the delusionary vision and all from a Royal, clearly the black sheep of the family, he thought, family with roots in Germany.

"Thank you for the call," he said politely, "and the best of luck." He wanted to add you will need it, but the gentleman he was, he decided not to.

The Prince, the apparent heir to the British throne, was stunned. Never had he received such brash treatment, not even from another Royal. Those German bastards, he thought, would never learn, two World Wars clearly had not taught them a lesson.

He was still furious as he met his mother for tea only one hour later. The Prince knew he had to control his emotion, his mother despised anger, but she had to hear the results of the phone call he had made to Berlin at once. The Queen always wanted to hear news at once, particularly bad news.

After tea with her son the Queen summoned her Prime Minister to Buckingham Palace. It was urgent, the P.M.'s Chief of Staff told her boss.

"She wants to meet with you now."

"Of course," the P.M. replied, "meetings with her Majesty are always urgent." She responded sarcastically.

"Please, call the Palace and let them know I will be there in one hour."

Buckingham Palace, originally known as Buckingham House, is the London residence and administrative headquarters of the reigning monarch of the United Kingdom. Originally the palace was a large town house built for the Duke of Buckingham in 1703. Later it became the private residence of Queen Charlotte and then was known as the "Queen's House."

During the 19th century it was enlarged and became the London residence of the British monarch in 1837. The building now has 775 rooms and the garden is the largest private garden in London.

The Queen met her Prime Minister in the "1844 Room" named after a visit by Tzar Nicholas of Russia to Queen Victoria that year. Both women were alone. The P.M. was on time. A single tea service had been placed on one of the tables, tea for her Prime Minister, the Queen had already enjoyed hers, not really enjoyed it for the news her son had brought to their meeting had not allowed her to enjoy her customary tea hour.

The Queen was direct, sharing the phone call her son had made to Prince Wilhelm, the President of the European Union.

Margaret Sawyer, the P.M. of Britain, listened carefully, showed no emotion, asked no questions.

"What do you think we should do about it?" the Queen asked.

Margaret reached for her tea cup and took a small sip.

"Clearly, Your Highness, you have a plan that's why you asked me to come, to see what I think about it."

This irritated the Queen, it was her P.M.'s demeanor, her rudeness, her subdued disrespect for the royal family. The Queen had never liked her Prime Minister, but her people did. The Prime Minister was extremely popular with Her Majesty's subjects, the people of Great Britain.

"You are right," the Queen responded, putting all her animosity aside, "you have told me that the reentry of my country is a matter of survival, and survival calls for extreme measures."

Margaret almost smiled, my country, she thought, the Royal family still believed all belonged to them, not our country, but my country, the arrogance, Margaret thought.

"It is quite clear to me," the Queen continued, "there is one hurdle we need to cross. You probably don't know that as a child I was a fair athlete, track and field, 100 meter hurdles was my event."

Margaret Sawyer tried the impossible, tried to envision in her mind the Queen jumping over hurdles. It was a picture even her intelligent mind would not let her see.

"And you need to know, whenever you could not jump the hurdle, when you were too fatigued or simply did not have the form, you had to kick the hurdle down to reach the finish line."

"Do you understand where I am going?" the monarch asked, disturbed, irritated by the one way conversation.

"Well, do you?" the Queen repeated.

"No", Margaret lied, she knew all too well, but she wanted the person who was convinced she had inherited all the superior genes, the genes that mattered, the genes that made her a Royal, a person better than anyone else, she wanted Her Majesty to say the words, words only Commoners would use. Margaret wanted her Queen to know that she was no different from anyone of her subjects. A lesson her Majesty had not learned for more than eighty years.

The Queen was clearly irritated by now, but she had learned over the years to never show her emotions. Is it possible my Prime Minister cannot follow a train of thought, understand my innuendos, understand where I am going? Yes, she decided, after all Margaret Sawyer was but a Commoner.

"OK", the Queen continued, "I will be straight forward, my story about knocking down a hurdle if you cannot cross it, to reach your goal, was but a metaphor, refers to one thing by mentioning another," she added with a smile clearly knowing her P.M. knew the meaning of a metaphor. After all, Margaret had graduated from Oxford, one of Britain's best universities.

"Thank you, Your Highness," Margaret Sawyer replied gently. She knew how to play the game, after all she was a politician, and one of the best in Great Britain. Again she picked up her cup of tea which was but luke warm and took another sip. Then she leaned back in her chair looking her Royal Highness straight in the eye. She waited.

The Queen accepted the stare for only a few seconds. There was no way to escape, she had to put her plan in simple words, in Commoner's language, her Prime Minister had forced her to do so.

"Fine," she said, now anxious to share her plan, to get the meeting over with.

"The hurdle we cannot cross is Prince Wilhelm, so we have to knock it down."

"Knock it down?" the Prime Minister asked, pleased she had once again made her Queen leave her comfort zone, giving her no alternative but to speak openly, directly, the way Commoners do.

"Yes," the Queen continued, realizing that she had underestimated her Prime Minister, "we need to knock down the hurdle, we need to eliminate Prince Wilhelm."

The Queen had anticipated a reaction, perhaps only a small one because she now knew her Prime Minister was a very cool customer. But there was none. Instead, Margaret Sawyer poured herself another cup of tea. The idea to assassinate Prince Wilhelm was not strange to her. After all assassinations were part of politics and she had ordered the death of one of her own, the Chief of MI6. Margaret also had decided that killing the President of the European Union was the only way for Britain to reenter the Union, for Britain to survive. Now she knew it was time for her to take the initiative, to let the Queen know who really was in control. The game was over.

"I agree," she responded to the surprise of the Queen, "and I know how to do it. It can never be us, MI6, it has to be done by a professional, by the best, and I know the man!"

CHAPTER XXXII

THE KREMLIN, MOSCOW

The president of Russia looked south out of the window of his luxurious office overlooking the Moscow River, the river whose waters ran through central Moscow and would eventually reach the Caspian Sea.

Although his favorite retreat was his dacha in Sochi almost 1000 miles away, here at the Kremlin, he always sensed his power, after all it was here where all the Tsars, the former monarchs had ruled. The Kremlin, built between 1492 and 1497, is the official residence of the President of the Russian Federation. Kremlin actually means a fortress inside a city, it was built between 1492 and 1495. It encompassed an area of more than 80 acres, surrounded by a wall 2444 yards long, the thickness of the wall varying between 3.5 and 6.5 meters. The complex includes five palaces, four cathedrals. Its walls and towers had been built by Italian masters, and its centerpiece is the Cathedral of Dormition where all the Tsars had been crowned.

Pavlov always arrived here in his helicopter, a Mil MI-8 helicopter, a twin engine machine.

As he looked at the river he knew he needed to do more. Yes, he thought cyberwarfare had been successful, it had achieved one of his strategic goals, to undermine the validity of America's election. The tactic had also worked in the Ukraine spreading chaos around the vote there. It was his strategic goal to undermine the validity of elections, his message was clear, no one is democratic. He believed that a perfectly thriving state can be transformed into an arena of fierce armed conflict. But unlike the chief of his general staff he did not believe it should be done within a matter of months.

And, he was impatient. He needed results now. As he paced his spacious office, where Tsars and Lenin had once made decisions which had changed the world, he too decided Prince Wilhelm was the major obstacle to make Russia great once again. The European Union had to be destroyed and cyberwarfare would take too long. He had to use the method he had used so successfully when he was the head of the KGB, methods he still used effectively. He decided that the head of the European Union, the Chancellor of Germany, had to be eliminated.

Vladimir Pavlov strolled towards his antique, wooden bar, and poured himself a Vodka, a Vodka on ice. As he took a glass he once more walked towards the large window overlooking the Moshova River. Clearly the job could not be done by his FSO, the Federal Protective Service, assigned to protect him or the FSB, the Federal Security Service, the successor of the KGB. No, he thought, he needed someone else, a professional killer, the best. And then he remembered the man he had met in his Mercedes limousine at the airport in Berlin.

10 DOWNING STREET, LONDON ENGLAND

Margaret Sawyer was pleased. She had very much enjoyed her meeting with her Majesty, the Queen of England. She had played the game, letting her Majesty know that royalty was no better than all the commoners, and she had succeeded. Of course Margaret knew her royal Majesty was right, the only way to gain reentry was to kick down the last hurdle, as her Queen had put it, assassinate Prince Wilhelm.

She paced her office at Downing Street Number 10, as it was colloquially known, the headquarters of Her Majesty's government, the official residence and office of the First Lord of the Treasury, a post held by the Prime Minister. The building was over 300 years old, contained 100 rooms and a private residence on the 3rd floor. There is a small garden half an acre, at her rear of the building. Ironically, Margaret thought, the first occupant to live here was Count Buthner, a German, an advisor to George I and George II.

Margaret summoned her Chief of Staff.

"I just met with the Queen," she said calmly. "She wants us to kick down the last hurdle, as she had put it."

"Kick down the last hurdle?" her Chief of Staff asked, not understanding the meaning.

"Yes," Margaret replied without emotion. "She wants us to assassinate Prince Wilhelm."

Her Chief of Staff was shocked.

"How,?" he asked in disbelief, "that is impossible."

"Not really," Margaret responded," clearly we cannot do it, not MI6, it has to be an outsider, a professional, the best. You know the man. We have used him once before. But I have decided to wait. The race has just begun, no need to kick down any hurdles, not yet anyhow."

THE WHITE HOUSE, WASHINGTON, D.C.

She never felt comfortable living at 1600 Pennsylvania Avenue, in NW Washington, D.C. She did not like the building built between 1792 and 1800. She knew all Presidents of the United States have lived there ever since John Adams first took occupancy on November 1, 1800. Since then it has been the residence of every President.

The house she thought was much too small for the most powerful person in the world, smaller than many other houses in her country. The house is located on 18 acres, only 55,000 square feet consisting of the Executive Suite, the West and East Wing and the Eisenhower Executive office building which now houses Offices for her and her VP's staff, and Blair House, a guest residence.

She sat in the Oval Office, the official office of the President of the United States, in the West Wing of the White House complex. The fireplace at the north end of the office was lit. It always was. Margaret Sawyer loved a roaring fire. And all the four doors had been opened, the east doors to the Rose Garden and the doors to her private library.

She sat alone behind Lincoln's desk. She was confused, for but a moment.

She wished her husband was there to consult her. But he had gone off on a trip with a bunch of his buddies. A guy trip, he had called it. Of course, she could contact him, ask for his advice, but she decided against it. Now she was the Commander-in-Chief, the President of the United States.

Although it was late, she called for her Chief of Staff, Roger Keifer. Roger, it seemed, never slept. Within less than 30 minutes he entered the Oval Office dressed in a pinstriped suit, a white shirt and blue tie.

"Please Roger, sit down. I have given a great deal of thought about the Brexit issue. If our intelligence is correct, and I am convinced it is, that Mr. Pavlov is orchestrating the demise of the European Union to change the balance of power, then we must stop him."

"I fully agree," Roger Kiefer responded, relieved that his President finally saw the big picture.

"If the E.U. ceases to exist it will enhance Russia's position as a world power and weaken ours."

"Then Mr. Pavlov must be stopped, and there is only one way it can be done. He must be eliminated."

Roger Keifer was not surprised, he too had come to that conclusion.

"But Roger, let me be clear about this, there can be no connection to us, none to our government."

"Of course," Roger replied, fully knowing his President was the best at concealing facts.

"Then," the President continued, "how will you do it?"

"Madam President, there is only one man who can do the job. He is a professional killer, an American. We have never used him, there will be no trace to us, but he is expensive."

"Expensive, what do you mean?"

"Thirty million dollars, I think perhaps more."

"That is a small price to pay to maintain our position in the world. I am sure the taxpayers will not mind," the President of the United States of America responded. Of course they would never know how the money was spent like most of their hard earned money the Internal Revenue Service always eagerly collected.

"Hire him!"

CHAPTER XXXIII

BEIGHT RASH, HAMEMSHELLA, 9 SMOLENSHIN STREET, JERUSALEM

The Prime Minister of Israel, Baron von Rosenberg, sat in his office in the upscale neighborhood of Rehavia in Jerusalem, in a building created by the Jewish German architect Richard Kaufmann in 1936. The Baron knew he had made the right decision. Israel needed to be part of the E.U., could no longer trust the United States of America.

Israel needed help, it was an island surrounded by enemies, he knew. Israel needed an ally committed to its survival. He had always worried about his best ally, the U.S.A, he knew that as many Jews lived in the U.S.A. as in Israel, six million. But recent US policies, the nuclear Iran deal, greatly concerned him, and the now President of the U.S. has supported it, in spite of all his objections.

Now Israel was more vulnerable than ever. He had known he needed a plan B. A plan that did not rely on the United States for his country's survival. That is why he had decided to become a Permanent member of the European Community, that's why he had decided to join Prince Wilhelm's concept to establish a new, strong, E.U., Russia, Germany, Austria and Israel. It was Israel's survival he had to protect.

He picked up his telephone, his secure line to the head of the Mossad, his intelligence agency.

"Maza," he said calmly, "fully cooperate with the man, you know who I mean and we will pay him whatever he asks."

"Understood," a click, the phone call was over.

VIENNA, AUSTRIA, BALLHAUSPLATZ 2

The Chancellor of Austria, the Kanzler, Werner von Habsburg, sat in his office deep in thought. He had just been informed about the details of the man to kill the President of the Russian Federation. He knew Prince Wilhelm was waiting for his approval. It was a difficult decision, but Werner had no alternative. For a moment he considered taking the short walk to the Hofburg Palace, the former imperial palace of Vienna, now the official residence of the President of Austria, to consult with the President. Although the President of Austria was but a ceremonial position, Werner respected the President. But quickly he decided against it. He realized it was a decision he, and only he, needed to make. Although he trusted the President, he concluded only as few people as possible should be involved. Werner decided to agree with Prince Wilhelm's plan. He contacted him at once.

CAPRI, ITALY

Adam stepped onto Victorino's gozzo at Marina Piccola on the island of Capri and hugged his old friend. Victorino was surprised, Adam did not wear his usual attire for a gozzo boat trip, a bathing suit, a loose linen shirt and sandals. Today he wore white linen slacks, a navy blue Polo shirt tucked into his pants, and white SeaVees shoes.

"Victorino," he said, "don't start the motor yet, don't pull out. I would like a glass of my favorite white wine first." Victorino nodded and opened the large, white cooler that contained the beverages. He rummaged through it searching for Adam's favorite white wine, a Pinot Grigio. But to his surprise, there was none.

"Sorry, Adam," Victorino exclaimed, embarrassed. "I have no Pinot Grigio."

"It's ok," Adam said, "serve me whatever you have, and please join me."

That's when Adam saw the bottle Victorino retrieved from the cooler, a bottle of Gruner Veltiner, the message from Prince Wilhelm. It was a go.

Victorino opened the bottle and poured a generous glass for Adam, a very small one for himself, he needed to be sober, he needed to captain the gozzo.

"Salute," Adam said and both glasses made contact.

"Salute," Victorino replied. Both took a drink from their glasses.

"Victorino, let's cancel the trip today."

"Why," the captain of the gozzo asked, "is it the wine? I am sorry."

"No, no, not at all, "Adam laughed, "I just changed my mind." He put down his glass on the small wooden chart table next to the helm station. Then he hugged Victorino.

"We will do it another day, soon, I promise."

He turned, stepped off the boat and began to ascend the steep stairs which led to his apartment.

Victorino was surprised. It had to be the wine, he would scold his wife for not having remembered Adam's favorite beverage. It was his wife that was responsible for all the supplies on his gozzo, the drinks, and the food. Suddenly he realized that Adam never intended to take the trip today, it was his clothing that gave it away. Victorino took a sigh, a sigh of relief.

Adam hastened up the steep steps taking two a time. The walk was circuitous, to minimize the steepness. After the first step he almost ran into the man, a young man, tall, muscular, short cropped hair, dressed in blue jeans, a white, short sleeved shirt not tucked into his pants, black loafers.

"I am sorry," Adam said.

"No problem, sir," the man responded, "may I have a word with you?"

Then Adam knew, the man was not there by accident, the man clearly was American, both his dress and his accent gave it away. A man from the Midwest, Adam surmised, but more importantly, a man from one of America's secret service agencies. Adam knew the type, after all, not too long ago he had been one of them.

"Of course", Adam replied. "But I am in a hurry. Why don't you walk up the stairs with me?"

"No problem," the man replied. "I have a message, more a request, a favor from Langley."

Adam was right, he usually was when it came to the spy business, his business.

"I'll be direct, that is what my boss told me to do, Pistol Pete, the head of the CIA. I think you know him."

Adam did not answer, but continued to walk up the stone stairs.

"We want to hire you for a job," the CIA man continued, "if you are interested, please call my boss, here is his number."

He handed Adam a small piece of paper turned and walked down the steep walkway. Adam took the paper, did not look at it, and pushed it into the right back pocket of his white linen pants. Another job, he thought, as he rushed up the stairs to his apartment building, eager to tell Nicole about his meeting with the CIA man. He would not tell her about the wine, the Gruener Veltiner.

MOSCOW, THE KREMLIN

Victor Molatov, the director of the Russian Presidential Security Service, part of the FSO, the federal protective service of Russia, had been instructed by Vladimir Pavlov to arrange for a meeting with Adam Bergman. The President of Russia had been clear, he wanted to meet with Adam again, the man he had first met in the Mercedes limousine at Berlin's airport. The meeting was to take place at Vladimir's dacha in Sochi. The meeting had to be secret.

Victor Molatov had done his homework. He knew all about the American assassin, the man trained by the Mossad and the NSA, knew that Adam had once been hired to protect the Chancellor of Germany, the President of the European Union, Prince Wilhelm. Knew about Nicole, his favorite gozzo trips in Capri, knew every detail about his upbringing, knew about his friendship with Maza Sharif, the head of the Mossad. And he knew all about Adam's daily routine on Capri, his six mile run every morning, early, before he had breakfast.

Victor decided to send one of his best agents to Capri, a woman, a young, beautiful woman Adam surely would not ignore. And he also knew Adam was for hire.

CHAPTER XXXIV

CAPRI, ITALY

Adam had a restless night. Earlier in the day, over lunch, Adam had told Nicole about his meeting with the CIA man, and showed Nicole the small piece of paper that contained the telephone number of her former boss, the chief of the CIA.

Both had been enjoying one of their favorite meals, scallopini al limone, boiled potatoes, carrots and peas. Nicole had urged him to call Langley to find out what the CIA wanted. But Adam was not sure, he had a full plate, a plate he had not shared with Nicole.

Adam rose early, put on his Nike shoes, his running shorts and shirt and left his apartment at 6:30 a.m., his routine. He first headed downhill towards the Marina Grande where soon all the cruise ships would arrive bringing hundreds of tourists to his island. Then he turned and headed uphill towards Ana Capri. It was a steep hill, the workout he always looked for. Then he saw her, how could he not. She was beautiful, blonde, young, with an athletic body. She was running towards him, gave him an enticing smile and then she fell, hit the ground hard. Adam immediately stopped and rushed towards her.

"Are you OK?" he asked as he helped her stand up.

"Yes, thank you", she said, her accent clearly British.

"Perhaps I should call you a taxi?" Adam responded.

"No thank you," she said, a broad smile on her face, "really, I am fine." Now she handed him a piece of paper, the message from her boss, Victor Molatov, the director of the Russian Presidential Security Service. She smiled again, turned and ran down the steep hill.

Unlike the way he had initially ignored the message from the CIA man only a day ago, Adam looked at the paper immediately. Mr.Pavlov, Russia's President wanted to meet at his dacha in Sochi in three days. A Fedex package will arrive at your apartment this afternoon. It contains all the travel information, the necessary passports. Please tell no one, our eyes are on you.

Adam knew he had to destroy the message as soon as possible. He headed back down the hill and entered the Quisisana Hotel, and asked the concierge for a book of matches. Then he entered one of the bathrooms a few steps up from the lobby, and burned the message.

Adam was elated, he needed to contact his friend Maza Sharef at the Mossad at once. But he had to be careful, very careful for now he knew Russia's eyes were on him. But he knew he would find a way. He must, because now he could go to Sochi, now he could be "Wild Bill", now he could pull the trigger.

Maza and Adam had agreed on the signal, Adam would send Maza to let him know all was a go, six bottles of Gruener Veltiner delivered to Maza's office. It was a plan they had developed while enjoying their trip on Victorino's gozzo. And twelve bottles, a full case, meant Adam had found a way to pull the trigger.

As soon as Adam returned to his apartment he asked Nicole for a favor.

"What is it?" she asked.

"You know my friend Maza Sharef, today is his birthday. I forgot all about it. I need to send him a present."

"What do you want to send him?" Nicole asked.

"One case of Gruener Veltiner, he really liked the wine when he visited us last."

"OK, how do I do it?"

"Simple," Adam replied, "you know Sappilo's our favorite wine store. They have a service like FTDE, where you can send flowers all over the world, well they really don't send them. They simply contact a store in whatever city that is part of the system. It is just a telephone call and the flowers, in our case, the wine will be delivered within an hour."

"OK," she said, "I'll do it right after you prepare my favorite breakfast."

"Thanks," Adam said, then held her tight and kissed her on the mouth.

The Fedex envelope arrived at 1 pm. It contained all the information of Adam's travel to Sochi, all fake passports that would leave no trace. Adam Bergman would never leave Italy.

TEL AVIV, ISRAEL

Maza received the message in the late afternoon. Twelve bottles of Gruener Veltiner, a full case, was delivered to his office.

Adam now was Wild Bill, he would pull the trigger. Maza had no idea how Adam would gain access to the target, the Russian President, that the target had invited the shooter to come to him. But Maza now knew his two agents who had infiltrated the FSO needed to act. They needed to plant the three small but powerful bombs in the horses, Adam would have no time for it. Each of the three horses needed a separate code to be dialed on the cell phone to detonate the bomb. Codes that Adam and Maza had agreed upon on their gozzo boat ride in Capri. No need to kill all three horses, just the horse the President of Russia was riding. Maza and Adam loved horses. Codes that Adam and the Maza had agreed upon on their gozzo boat ride in Capri.

CHAPTER XXXV

CAPRI, ITALY

Adam wanted for Nicole to have no part of it. It was too dangerous a mission, a mission he may not survive. He decided to send Nicole abroad, back to the United States. Both had long discussions about the message the CIA agent had handed Adam. Nicole had urged him to call her former boss, pistol Pete, to learn all about. But Adam knew it was not the right play, he had a mission to fulfill, a mission that could change the balance of power in the world.

After the long discussions he had convinced Nicole to go back to Langley, meet her former boss, find out what was on his mind. After all, Adam had argued, we are a team, and you, Nicole, are as much part of it as I. Finally, she had agreed. And when Adam suggested she should also visit her family in Cleveland, who she had not seen in almost two years, she agreed. She booked a flight the very next day.

ROME TO WASHINGTON

Adam was relieved. He did not want to tell Nicole he had to leave Capri for several days, lying about where he was going. No more need, now he had the elbow room he needed.

Adam also decided not to tell Prince Wilhelm of his good fortune, that the president of Russia had invited him to his dacha. No need to. Adam had a job to do and if and when it was done the aftermath was not his business, it was Prince Wilhelm's and the other Royals'.

Adam did make the phone call to his bank in the Cayman Islands. Yes, he was told all the money had been wired into his account. Adam decided not to take Nicole to their favorite restaurant for their last dinner before she flew back to the U.S., perhaps their last dinner ever. Instead he cooked himself, prepared Nicole's favorite dish. First he served Cristal champagne on the terrace of his luxurious apartment. It was a beautiful night, a full moon, stars close enough to touch. Then he had prepared escargot served with white toast. The main course was a rack of lamb, Nicole's favorite. He had prepared no dessert, Nicole never ate dessert, but both enjoyed a Grapa.

That night they made love as if it had been the first time. They explored, kissed, the best love they had ever made. The next morning Adam prepared Nicole breakfast, the breakfast she loved, O.J., black coffee, two eggs over light, white toast, and bacon. After breakfast Adam walked Nicole to the taxi-stand. He placed her suitcase in the trunk, opened the rear door, held her tight and kissed her passionately. He knew he would miss her.

The cab slowly entered the narrow street which led to the Marina Grande where Nicole would board the ferry to Naples. Adam leisurely walked back to his apartment. He was alert now wondering if Russia's eyes were watching. He saw no one, but he was wrong.

Adam had time, another day before his journey to Sochi. When he entered his apartment he poured himself another cup of coffee. He took the cup and sat down in the reclining chair on his terrace. He took a sip of the coffee. This mission, his mission, was very unusual. Adam always liked to survey where the kill was to take place, learn all the surroundings, all the possible getaways. But this time he would have no such knowledge, and he knew there was no getaway, he would be in Russia surrounded by the Russian secret service. This time he had to improvise, shooting from the hip. He had never done it before, all his kills had always been carefully planned, meticulously laid out, each move anticipated, all full proof. But not this time. Adam did not mind. He loved the challenge. He thought he could do it.

CHAPTER XXXVI

SOCHI, RUSSIA

The trip was long, but it was easy, all arrangements had been made. When Adam stepped off the ferry in Naples a limousine was waiting for him, and took him to the Airport. He did not wait in line, he had a diplomatic passport. The flight from Naples to Budapest, Ferenc Liszt International, was uneventful, as was his flight to Moscow's SVO, Sheremetyevo, airport. Adam now was a Hungarian diplomat attending a meeting in Moscow. But at Moscow's airport he never reached a gate, instead a black limousine with a driver and two security men took him to a large private jet already on the runway, ready to take off.

The plane was luxurious, appointed with leather seats, couches, even a bedroom, and a bathroom with a shower. Only eight people boarded the plane, two pilots, three flight attendants, two FSB agents and Adam. The plane left as soon as Adam had taken a seat. Even before it had reached cruising altitude the flight attendants, all young, all pretty, swarmed all over him. At first there was Champagne and caviar, then vodka on ice, followed by a delicious, elaborate lunch. Now, he thought, this is living. Adam knew Soci was approximately

1900 miles from Moscow, a three and half hour flight, a flight he had every intention to enjoy.

The attractive flight attendants clearly had been instructed to entertain Adam. After the food was served they all made a special effort to get him involved in a conversation. Adam enjoyed it. The FSO agents had taken a seat in the back of the plane and never spoke. They were served no food. Russia does not seem to be all that bad, Adam thought with a snicker.

Adam knew little about Sochi, he had never visited the city on the black sea. He knew it had approximately 34500 inhabitants, and a 145 kilometers shoreline where most people lived. Its climate is subtropical, mild winters with average temperatures of 52 degrees Fahrenheit and warm summer temperatures ranging in the mid seventies. He also knew that his host, Vladimir Pavlov, was not the first Russian leader to love Sochi, Joseph Stalin had his favorite dacha, a second home, built there.

The large private jet landed at Sochi International Airport at 5:33 PM local time. It taxied to a private hangar at the south end of the Airport. There three black limousines were waiting. As Adam exited the plane and touched Russian soil, a small, older man dressed in a black suit greeted him. He shook Adam's hand.

"Welcome to Sochi," he said in fluent english. "My name is Victor Molatov, I hope you had a pleasant flight."

"I did, thank you," Adam replied, fully knowing that Victor Molatov was the head of the Russian president's security.

"Please," Victor continued," follow me and join me in my car. I will take you to the president's dacha. Of course, he won't be able to see you tonight but arrangements have been made for a lunch meeting tomorrow."

"That's great," Adam replied," I need some sleep. It was a long trip."

"Of course, Mr. Bergman, you will be staying in one of the guest houses, very comfortable, and I've assigned one of my people to see to every one of your needs."

"Thank you, very kind of you," Adam replied.

By now the car had reached the president of Russia's compound, a white, three story mansion overlooking the black sea. Residence Riviera or Riviera 6, as the estate is officially known, is located in Riviera Park, originally designed for the pleasure of Russians Tsars. As the large SUV had slowly approached the entrance of the park, Adam had noticed the large mosaic of Lenin at the end of the concrete walkway leading into the park. The monument had been dedicated to the staff of Sochi's hospitals where more than 0.5 million red army soldiers had been saved during world war two.

The dacha is magnificent, located near the beach. There are several other buildings, many small cottages. The car pulled up to a smaller cottage perhaps 100 yards from the large mansion. It was located right on the beach.

"This, Mr. Bergman will be your home. I hope it meets all your comforts."

"Thank you, and good night," Adam answered as he entered the cottage. The lodging was luxurious, a large living room, a library with a fireplace, three bedrooms each with a full bath and a fully equipped kitchen. The furniture was all Ralph Lauren. The terrace with a splash pool abutted the beach. I could live here, Adam thought. But it did not take long for reality to set in. Adam had barely unpacked his small suitcase when there was a knock on the door.

"Just a moment," Adam said as he stepped to open the door.

"Sir, I am sorry to disturb you but my chief thought you might enjoy a glass of wine before you turn in tonight."

"Well, yes, I do, very kind of you," Adam replied. Then he noticed the bottle among the ice cubes and the ice bucket, a bottle of Gruener Veltiner. Now he knew this man was one of Maza's men, one of the two katzas who had infiltrated the FSO.

"Please tell your chief I am very grateful. Have a good night."

"A good night," the man said," yes, I will have a good night. Thank you."

Then the man left. But now Adam knew all was in place, the bombs had been implanted in Vladimir Pavlov's favored horses, a "good night" was the agreed upon code words Maza and Adam had decided upon as they had drifted in the gozzo in the calm and peaceful bay of Naples. Although the bed in Adam's cottage was the most comfortable he had ever been in, he could not sleep. Tomorrow he would pull the trigger that would change the world.

CHAPTER XXXVII

SOCHI, RUSSIA

Adam rose early, 6 am. He would follow his routine, put on his running gear and leave his luxurious dacha. He crossed the terrace and stepped on to the beach to begin his 6 mile run. The water of the Caspian sea was calm, there was no wind, the beach was empty. Noone was following him, strange, he thought.

But Victor Malotov had instructed his FBO agents to leave Adam alone, to make him feel at ease, feel comfortable. After all, there was no place for him to go.

Adam ran along the beautiful beach, a soft breeze off the sea cooled his body, it invigorated him. It was the kind of day when he could run forever. But he knew today was not the day, he had a date, a date he could not break. It was a date with one of the most powerful people in the world, the President of the Russian Federation.

A table had been set up only a few feet from the main house, just beyond the large swimming pool. There were only two chairs, two table settings and two vodka glasses.

Adam had arrived early, 10 minutes early. He was dressed casually, his favorite white linen pants, a white linen shirt and white Seevees loafers. As he approached the table the President of Russia was already waiting for him. Adam was surprised, he knew Vladimir Pavlov had a reputation of always being late, always needing to be the last person to arrive.

Adam apologized.

"No need," the Russian oligarch responded smiling, as he motioned Adam to take the seat next to him. It was a beautiful day, no wind, the Caspian sea calm, not a cloud in the sky.

"I am very glad you came," the Russian continued. "I knew you would, I saw it in your eyes when we first met in my limousine at the Brandenburg airport in Berlin. You are very much like me, you love challenges and you love to dress in white," as he pointed to his white slacks and white sleeveless shirt. Both laughed.

"Please," the President continued, "let's eat. Have some of the world's best caviar from the Caspian sea and a glass of Russian vodka, a must."

Adam smiled, he loved caviar and he loved vodka.

The Russian President raised his glass. "Salute, here is to a new friendship."

"To our friendship," Adam echoed.

LANGLEY, VIRGINIA

William P. Davis was a large man, a six foot and three inch muscular frame, brown hair and dark brown eyes. Pistol Pete, as the Director of Central Intelligence, DCI, was affectionately known, sat in his large office on the seventh floor of the headquarters of America's Central Intelligence Agency. He leaned his large frame back into the antique swivel chair his wife had bought him at a flea market in Philadelphia.

The DCI was in deep thought, he knew he needed advice, but had no one to turn to. The subject matter had been classified "Eagle", the highest security clearance. Only the President and he were aware of the mission. He rose from the chair and strolled towards the small bar in one of the corners of his office. He retrieved a Diet Coke, his favorite drink and began to pace his luxuriously appointed office, antique furniture, a large Persian rug, a Rembrandt on the wall behind his desk.

All night he had not been able to sleep, all night he had thought about the President's order, the assassination of the President of the Russian Federation. And there was to be no trace to the USA. To kill the Russian President was an almost impossible task, to leave no trace to the US was impossible.

Pistol Pete decided to break all the rules, he had no choice. Slowly he picked up his telephone and called his long time friend on his secure line.

"Yes," Maza Sharef, head of the Mossad, Israel's renowned intelligence agency, answered.

"Maza," the DCI began, "I know I am breaking all the rules, but I desperately need your help."

"Shoot," Maza responded, "I am all yours."

"Well, this is classified "Eagle", do you know what that means?"

"Of course," Maza answered. His Mossad knew all.

"OK," the DCI continued, small beads of sweat forming on his forehead. He stepped towards his desk, put down the unopened can of Diet Coke, and continued.

"The President of my country wants to eliminate Vladimir Pavlov, the Russian President," he said almost in a whisper, afraid someone else could be listening.

"How will you do it?" Maza inquired calmly, showing no surprise, no emotion in his voice.

"That is why I am calling you, Maza. I don't know. I have thought about it, considered many options, but found no answer. And, of course, there can be no trace of us. I need your help."

"Fair enough," Maza replied calmly, already knowing the answer. "Let me think about it for a day or two, I am sure he does not have to die today."

"No, of course not," the DCI responded, surprised by his friend's composure, his matter of fact approach. But that was Maza, he reminded himself, that is why I trust him.

The phone call ended. Maza smiled. He knew that in a couple of days all would be taken care of. The Americans always seemed to be a step or two behind, and Maza liked it that way. But this time he was wrong, his friend, Pistol Pete, had already sent a messenger to Capri.

CHAPTER XXXVIII

WANNSEE, BERLIN, GERMANY

The Chancellor of Germany, the President of the EU Union, Prince Wilhelm von Hohenzollern, sat in his dark green rocking chair, a chair his family had owned for hundreds of years. It was late afternoon and the lake was calm, the lake where he had learned how to swim at the age of five. Here he always relaxed, thought about world politics, thought about his family, his ancestors.

He took a drink from his favorite beer, Charlottenburger Pils. He had not heard from Adam Bergman since he had sent the bottle of Gruener Veltiner to Victorino's gozzo. Prince Wilhelm was not concerned, Adam was a professional, Adam was the best.

THE AEGEAN SEA

Maria, the 250 foot yacht, was anchored only a few hundred meters off the island off Mykonos in the Aegean sea. The yacht had been named after his mother the Great Duchess of Russia, Grand Duke reminded himself. The Duke had convinced his family to leave Madrid and take a cruise on their yacht. He wanted everyone to be there when the news of the assassination of the President of the Russian Federation of Russia was announced, when he became the new leader of Russia.

His mother, Maria, Grand Duchess of Russia, knew nothing about the plot. But his father did. The Grand Duke was not sure of what was to happen after the assassination of the President of Russia. All he had been told, he would be the next President of the Russian Federation. The Grand Duke decided to wait and watch the events from his yacht, Maria.

VIENNA, AUSTRIA, BALLHAUSPLATZ 2

Austria's chancellor, Werner von Habsburg, knew the bottle of Gruener Veltiner had been sent. All had agreed to assassinate Vladimir Pavlov and all had agreed on the method. But no one had mentioned a follow up plan, what was to happen after the assassination.

As he walked towards his plain wooden desk he realized there was a follow up plan, there had to be. No doubt Prince Wilhelm had designed it, and was its architect. But why has he not shared the plan with me and the others? Perhaps I am the only one to be excluded, Austria's Chancellor wondered, always suspicious of the Hohenzollern.

LANGLEY, VIRGINIA

The phone on the protected line at the home of the DCI rang late in the evening. Already in his pajamas William P. Davis answered.

"Peter," it's me."

The DCI knew at once who the caller was. No one ever called him Peter, not even his wife. It was only his friend, Maza, the head of the Mossad.

"What's up?" the DCI asked."

"Sorry I am calling you so late, but I know you are anxious to get the answer regarding "Eagle."

"Yes, of course," the DCI said anxiously.

"Well, it will be taken care of in the very near future. No need for you to know any details, it is better you don't. The man, the best, is expensive and as he pointed out to me, this has to be his last job. Therefore he wants the following money transfers, half now, half after the job is done. The initial half is nonrefundable, no matter what the outcome. One hundred and fifty million dollars sent to Swiss Raiffeisen, account no.: 1943007."

"Done," the DCI responded and hung up the phone.

CHAPTER XXXIX

SOCHI, RUSSIA

The lunch had been one of the best Adam had ever had, and he enjoyed the host Vladimir Pavlov. Adam thought he was the kind of guy I could hang around with, not only likeable but one of the guys.

The President of the Russian Federation felt the same. He liked Adam, a man like him, but he also knew Adam was an assassin, a man for hire, one you can never trust.

"Adam", he said, "I asked you to come here for a purpose. I really like you, let's go out tonight, let's have fun, I want to get to know you better."

"Fun is what I am all about," Adam responded.

Vladimir Pavlov had decided to wait, to learn more about the person he had sent for. A night in Sochi, he decided, could tell all.

It did, both men bonded, both men became friends, not the kind of friend you trust over years, but the man you look in the eye, the hand shake, the man you knew you could trust. A mistake the former head of the KGB had never made before.

Both men met again for breakfast at Riviera 6, Mr. Pavlov's dacha. Both men had enjoyed the previous night, visiting several night clubs in Sochi, partying, and dining.

"Adam", Vladimir began the conversation. By now, after partying and dining, both men were on a first name basis, "Adam", he continued," this afternoon, after lunch, I want to tell you why I sent for you. But first let's take a ride on my horses along the beach. Do you like to ride?"

"Vladimir, I love it, it is one of my passions, only second to women."

"OK", the President continued,"we'll use my best horses. Let's meet at 11am on the beach."

"Great", Adam replied, fully knowing that his three best horses had been implanted with the bomb, the bomb designed to kill the President of the Russian Federation.

"Adam, by the way, only wear a bathing suit. That's the way I like to ride on the beach", he said with a broad grin.

There had been rumors spread by the western media, mostly American media, about Mr. Pavlov's sexual preference. But Adam knew Vladimir had clearly shown his hand as they had partied most of the night in the nightclubs of Sochi, like Adam Vladimir loved women!

Adam was punctual, actually 10 minutes early. To his surprise and contrary to his reputation, the President of the Russian Federation was already waiting on the beach.

As Adam approached him both men shook hands, smiled. Both men clad in only Speedo bathing suits, showed their muscular bodies. Both were athletes, thin, firm, not an ounce of fat.

Vladimir Putin had the reins of two of the best horses he had ever set eyes on, a stallion and a mare.

"Adam", he said. "It is your choice. These are the best horses, Chloe and Fin, you choose."

Adam knew a small bomb had been implanted in both of the horses. He hesitated, for but a moment, feigning making a decision.

"I'll take Fin, if you don't mind."

"Thank you," the Russian President responded. "Actually, Chloe is my favorite. How did you know?"

Adam hesitated, a thousand thoughts coming to his mind, did the Russian President know?

"Well," Adam responded with a grin. "I just know you like the female gender, and Chloe is a mare."

Vladimir laughed as he mounted his favorite horse. Both Adam and he would ride bareback along the now deserted beach. But both would not be alone. Two FSO agents rode fifty yards in front, two fifty yards behind.

The signal Adam and Maza had agreed upon was simple. Adam would raise both of his arms letting Mr Pavlov know that he enjoyed the ride. Then Maza's agent, one of the men who had infiltrated the FSO, one who sat on the terrace of Adam's cottage, would enter the code that was on his cell phone, the code that would detonate the small, but powerful bomb in Chloe's body.

Usually the President of Russia loved to let the horse gallop along the beach, along the shallow water. Today he did not. Today he trotted slowly next to Adam, he wanted to talk to him. The FSO agents, two ahead, two behind, followed.

Adam knew that the remote detonator, the cell phone held by the Mossad agent on the terrace of his cottage, had a limited range. He also knew that Mr. Pavlov was too close to him, a bomb detonated now, at this distance, could kill him. But Adam knew now was the moment.

"Let's race," he said and put both of his heels into his magnificent horse. Then raised his arms.

The explosion was devastating. Chloe and her rider flew 10 feet into the air, and when they landed on the beach and in the shallow water, there were only body parts, arms, legs, intestines of a human and a horse intermingled, indistinguishable. Blood everywhere, staining the Black Sea at the shore.

The President of Russia had died instantly riding his favorite horse, Chloe. But the blast from the bomb also had catapulted Adam 20 feet into the water of the Black Sea. His horse, unhurt and full of fear, raced down the beach.

At first, for but for a second, there was complete silence, all in disbelief. Then the FSO, the President of Russia's security service, jumped into action. Two of the people on horseback raced to where their President, or his remains were tangled with the corpse of his favorite horse. The other two raced for Adam who was lying face down in the Black Sea, unconscious.

Both FSO agents pulled Adam's body onto the beach, turned him, and one began mouth to mouth respiration. That's when Adam regained consciousness, when he spit out much of the sea water. He began to breathe again. At first he did not feel the pain of his compound fractured left fibula, the fracture of his left humerus, the rib fractures. Trauma initially always acts as an anesthetic. But Adam's breathing was painful, labored.

The ambulance from the MBHC - Municipal Budgetary Healthcare Institution of Sochi, City Hospital no.4 arrived within minutes. Adam was placed in the back of an ambulance and then it raced towards 42 Dagonysskaya Street in Sochi. The hospital is Sochi's best, 655 beds, and two trauma surgeons on call.

Adam was taken immediately to the first floor, the surgical department where X Ray facilities including CT were available.

After a brief, but thorough evaluation the damage had been assessed, a fracture of the left humerus, a compound fracture of his left tibia, plus fractures of several left ribs, and a 40 percent pneumothorax of his left lung, a collapsed lung.

The trauma surgeon had quickly inserted a Heimlich tube into Adam's left chest cavity to expand his lung. Now the orthopedic surgeons took over, cast along his left arm, cast along his left leg, fluids, antibiotics to ward off any infection.

At first Adam had been admitted to a 6 bed intensive care unit. Clearly only precautions because Adam's condition was by no means critical. The next day, at the request of Victor Moletov, the head of FSO, Mr. Pavlov's personal security force, Adam was moved into a private wing of the hospital.

A wing that had been designated for the President of Russia in the event he took ill.

As Adam awoke after the heavy sedation that the doctors had administered, he thought he had died and now was in heaven. He glanced up and saw the room filled with flowers. Clearly, heaven, Adam thought.

And then he saw his face, only inches away.

"Adam," the President of Russia whispered, "Adam, I am so sorry, please forgive me. My protection has failed you. I will do everything to find out what went wrong. Today I was unable to ride with you, yet I did not want to disappoint you. I sent my double, I have several of them. Unfortunately he died. But, thank God, you survived. I will make sure you will receive the best care, you are my friend, the friend I always searched for. I will never forgive myself, I am deeply sorry. If you have any need, any wish, please let me know. Also, Adam, let's keep this between us, let the world think I am dead. Let's see what will crawl out of the gutter."

Adam nodded his head. "I thought I was in heaven."

"You are," the President of Russia responded," you are in Sochi, Russia!"

CHAPTER XL

LANGLEY, VIRGINIA

The DCI,the director of Central Intelligence, Pistol Pete, gave Nicole a warm hug. Nicole had arrived in Washington, D.C. only a few hours ago. She had enjoyed her visit with her family in Cleveland, a trip Adam had recommended. It was here where she had learned about the assassination of the Russian President.

"Nicole," Pistol Pete said after both had taken a seat on the large, brown, leather couch in the DCI's luxurious office.

"Great,thank you, and my dad sends his regards."

Nicole's dad and the DCI had been best friends, roommates in college and in law school. It was the DCI who had convinced Nicole to join the CIA after her graduation from Yale's law school.

"Does he still play golf, is he still a hacker?"

"Yes," Nicole laughed," nothing has changed."

"Nicole," Pistol Pete continued, now more serious,"not long ago I sent a man to Capri to talk to Adam about an assignment."

"Well," Nicole said,"that's why I am here. Adam is busy but he wanted to respond quickly, that's why he sent me."

"I understand," Pistol Pete replied. "But now things have changed. The death of Russia's President has changed the mind of my boss, the President of the United States."

"How so?" Nicole asked anxiously.

"My President and the Premier of Great Britain had a meeting. Both view the rise of the EU, now that Russia could become part of it, as a threat to the balance of power. Both the US and Great Britain do not want a strong EU, an alliance that would challenge us not only economically but also militarily. They want to stop it."

"Stop it, how?" Nicole asked, fully knowing the answer."

"To put it simply," the DCI continued while taking a drink of his favorite beverage, a diet Coke, "they have decided to eliminate the President of the EU."

"Eliminate?" Nicole asked innocently, fully understanding the meaning.

"Yes," Pistol Pete continued," they want Prince Wilhelm to be assassinated, and they want the best to do it. They want Adam."

Nicole was not surprised. She knew for the CIA to summon Adam it had to be important.

"Nicole," the DCI went on, "I know you are partners, you are lovers and I trust you. Please deliver my message to Adam."

Nicole smiled. "Of course I will, and he will do it. He loves challenges."

Nicole rose from the leather sofa, gathered her purse, and was ready to leave.

"Nicole," Pistol Pete asked, "don't you want to know the price, doesn't Adam want to know?"

"Of course," Nicole answered.

"I have been authorized to pay 100 million Euros."

One hundred million Euros, Nicole was stunned. But it was not the money it was the challenge, the challenge both she and Adam loved. But she knew this was one challenge Adam would decline. After all, the Prince was a good friend and Adam had been hired to protect him. She was certain that this time Adam would say No. But why tell him, Nicole wondered, why did he have to know? That's when she decided that it would be her job, it was her time to be in charge. No longer would she play second fiddle to her lover, now she had the opportunity to become the world's number one assassin. After all she had been trained by the best, Adam. She knew all of Adam's methods, all his tricks, knew how to kill, knew how to make it look like the terrorists did it. She decided she did not need Adam any more. No need to split 100 million Euros.

"Uncle Pete," she said as she hugged the head of the CIA, "please transfer the money three days from now into my and Adam's joint account in the Cayman Islands."

"No problem, Nicole," he said as he kissed her on the cheek.

LAKE WANNSEE, BERLIN

Prince Wilhelm of Hohenzollern, Germany's chancellor, the President of the EU, sat in his small, wooden fishing boat which was tied to the dock attached to his boat house on lake Wannsee. He had rolled up the bottom of his pants, careful not to make them wet. His wife always insisted on it, she did not enjoy his wet pants often smelling of fish.

The lake was calm, not a single wave rocking his boat, it was a very peaceful evening, a full moon illuminating the lake. The Prince lit a cigar, his favorite cigar, a Padron torpedo. He did not inhale, never did, but he loved the taste of the tobacco.

The Prince reminisced, recalled all he had done rejuvenating Germany to once again be prosperous, be Europe's most powerful economic force, uniting 27 countries to be part of the European Union, making the EU one of the most powerful states in the world.

Finally, he was successful in completing his dream. Russia was now about to become a member of the European Union and his family, many of the Royals, were in control. He took another long draft from his cigar. Most importantly, he thought, he had prevented Great Britain from reentering the EU, Great Britain the black sheep of my family.

He knew he had to get back to the house and join his wife and their dinner guest, Adam Bergman. His wife had prepared Wiener Schnitzel, one of Adam's favorite dishes.

Adam and the wife of the Prince were sitting on the terrace overlooking the lake. The Prince's wife was sitting in her favorite rocking chair, a chair she had bought years ago at an auction in Charlottenburg.

As the Prince put his right foot on the wooden dock as he was disembarking from his small boat, the bomb exploded. The wooden boat flew into the air in many pieces as did the Prince. All landed in the shallow, calm water of lake Wannsee.

The Princes's wife was in shock, Adam put her into his arms, tried to calm her but she had fainted. By now all of the BND agents assigned to protect the President of Germany swarmed the place. Noone was to enter, noone was to leave. Then Adam took charge. The BND agents knew Adam had been hired to protect their President and he was to be in command. Adam instructed everyone that the true cause of death of the Prince could not be revealed. Officially the Prince died of a heart attack while having dinner at his home.

It did not take the BND and Adam long to determine how the Prince had been assassinated. It was a small but powerful bomb, Syntex, less than 50 grams, the size of a butter bar, which had been secured in a water proof plastic bag and fastened to the bottom of the small fishing boat. It was the signature bomb of the terrorist groups in the Middle East. Precisely the same tool and method Adam would have used. He had used the same bomb in the assassination attempt on the Russian President. Suddenly Adam's instinct told him that this was not the act of a terrorist group. Other than Maza, the head of the Mossad, he had never discussed with anyone how he had intended to kill Russia's President, or had he? Clearly the Mossad had no reason to kill the Prince, on the contrary, the Mossad was his ally. But who else? Then Adam remembered the long conversations he and Nicole frequently had on their terrace in Capri. Adam had always explained all the details of his kills, the details of the planning, the execution, what weapons best to use, all of his skills. Nicole had always been very attentive, always eager to learn. Over the last couple of years Adam had trained Nicole to become an assassin, his right hand. Nicole was intelligent, ambitious, she had learned quickly.

Of course, Adam thought, it had to have been Nicole who killed the Prince. Noone else knew all the details to accomplish this assassination. Noone knew Adam's plan on how to protect the Prince, no one knew the Prince's schedule, his daily habits, all the details necessary for an assassin to successfully complete the job. Yes, he thought, it was Nicole. Nicole apparently was about to get into the assassination business on her own. His business!

CHAPTER XLI

CAPRI, ITALY

It was Nicole's birthday. Nicole had asked Adam for a romantic day, a day just for the two of them. She knew Adam was most vulnerable during their love making when he was bare, full of emotions. Adam had agreed, I'll make all the arrangements, he had assured her, first a gozzo trip in Victorino's boat, then dinner at our favorite restaurant, then love making all night, he had proposed.

It was a plan that suited Nicole perfectly, an afternoon on the gozzo, a romantic dinner, love making to follow. Adam would be completely relaxed, not on guard, she was sure.

Nicole and Adam stepped down the stairs leading from their apartment to the small marina, Marina Piccola. Victorino's gozzo was docked there, bobbing gently in the calm sea. But there was no Victorino, no captain of the boat.

"Where is Victorino?" Nicole asked as she stepped into the boat.

"Nicole," Adam responded," this is a day for just you and I." He gently kissed her on the mouth. "I want to be alone with you, away from everyone, everything, be just with you."

Adam pushed the gozzo off the rocks of the Marina Piccolo and steered it expertly into the calm waters of the bay of Naples. He went further offshore than Victorino ever did.

"Adam," Nicole asked," why are we going so far offshore?"

"I want to be alone with you, make love to you in the boat."

By now the gozzo was a mile off shore, here the water was deep. Adam killed the motor and slowly walked towards Nicole who was relaxing on the lounge cushion in front of the boat. He lied on top of her, kissed her passionately, Nicole fully expecting that he was about to make love to her. Instead he reached for one of the many blue and white pillows scattered about the lounge cushion. He quickly and forcefully placed it on Nicole's face. She had no chance. She kicked, tried to throw him off, to no avail. His muscular body kept her pinned to the sun bed, his strong hands pushing the pillow so she could not breathe. The struggle did not last long. She suffocated.

Adam stood up, he did not have to feel Nicole's pulse, he knew she was dead. He walked back to the stern of the boat, opened a large locker and retrieved three items he had stored there earlier in the morning. The first was a Rocna stainless steel anchor weighing 88 pounds, the second was a heavy MarineNow ⅝" anchor chain, the third was a large, sturdy plastic bag. He had cut several holes in it to let the water enter it more rapidly.

He lifted the lifeless body of Nicole and placed it into the plastic bag. He then attached the chain to the anchor and fastened both to Nicole's body. The package was very heavy but Adam was strong and in one motion he tossed it into the sea of the bay of Naples. He had tied the free end of the chain to the boat, it was a long chain and several feet were still in the boat assuring Adam that the anchor had hit bottom. He walked back to the helm, started the engine and put the gear in forward. He was setting the anchor.

Once he was satisfied that the anchor was secured, he tossed the rest of the chain into the water and steered the boat back towards his home, Marina Piccola. Adam reached into the large white cooler of Victorino's gozzo and retrieved a bottle of his favorite wine, a Pinot Grigio. He poured a glass, then lit one of his favorite cigars, a Padron torpedo, anniversary edition. Yes, he thought, Nicole had been beautiful, intelligent, and wonderful in bed. But he knew there would be more. As he put the bottle of Pinot Grigio back into the cooler next to him, he noticed the bottle of Gruener Veltiner floating on top of the ice. He picked up the bottle and threw it into the calm water of the bay of Naples. No more Gruener Veltiner he thought with a smile.

SOCHI, RUSSIA

The Russian President sat on the beach in front of his dacha in Sochi. He was alone. In recent months he had seldom visited here fearing the drone strikes by the Ukrainians. But his lover had urged him to spend a few days on the beach, relax and be with each other.

He was dressed in only his favorite bathing suit, a black Speedo. Even though it was early in the morning he was enjoying a glass of Vodka. It made him relax, let him think more clearly, he thought. Clear thinking was what he needed right now. He knew that the invasion of the Ukraine, and his efforts to have Britain leave the European Union, had been a mistake. After all, the EU's leaders had welcomed Brexit and had vowed to keep them out of the EU permanently. Now Mr. Pavlov realized to make Russia great again, he needed a different strategy. Then he recalled the conversations he often had with the former chancellor of Germany. A bright woman educated in East Germany under communist rule. She had earned a Phd degree in nuclear chemistry and she spoke fluent Russian. She had always argued the benefits of a closer alignment between Germany and Russia.

He rose to his feet and began to pace the beach deep in thought. Yes, he wondered, closer ties to Germany may be the right strategy. If Russia were to join the European Union, the EU clearly would become the most powerful force on earth, both militarily as well as economically. And Russia would without doubt become the leader of the EU. After all, even a strong economic Germany relied on Russia for its energy. Yes, he thought with a spring in his step, joining the European Union will make Russia great again.

CHAPTER XLII

BERLIN, GERMANY

Prince Maximillian von Habsburg looked out of the large window of his office overlooking one of Berlin's magnificent parks, the Tiergarten. He reminisced. Noone could have predicted the chain of events that resulted because of Brexit, he thought. Unfortunately he had lost his best friend, a member of his family, Prince Wilhelm. Yet the EU had become stronger than ever. All thanks to Great Britain, he snickered.

He had done much to expand the EU, to strengthen it. Russia's and Israel's membership had solidified the union, made it a world power. But he knew he was not home free. It was the USA that was the EU's true enemy now. He began to pace his large office, he was deep in thought. Clearly the USA was trying to destroy the EU for a strong EU would change the balance of power, a balance the USA had no intention of changing.

Maximillian returned to his leather chair in the office of the chancellery in Berlin. The death of his best friend, Prince Wilhelm, had been a shock, a blow to the EU. But Max was determined to continue his friend's mission, a united Europe. All had agreed he should be the leader.

Only weeks ago he had accomplished his dream, his dream to once again make Austria and Germany one country. Max was a Habsburg, a diplomat, a strategist, always exploring the motives of all the players, and he had campaigned tirelessly against nationalism, reminding all the harm it had done in Europe in the past.

He knew all too well that the new President of the USA was calling for nationalism, America first, was his slogan. It was a bold call, Max thought, campaigning on nationalism. The USA is a nation of many colors, many religions. Yet after 150 years it had yelled into one nation, at least that had been the bet of the new President. Max, however, knew that the President of the USA did not believe in nationalism. He was an astute businessman and as Max he believed in globalization as the way of the future. But with Brexit the Brits again had made nationalism popular and the US President had bet on it. He was right, he handedly won the election.

Clearly, Max thought, nationalism may be right to win an election in America but it was not right for Europe and the rest of the world. Europe knew all about nationalism, it had been the cause of many wars, it had divided Europe. Max knew that national spirit was always strong in Europe, particularly in Britain, France and Germany. Germany had tried to suppress it because of its history. But now the new President of the USA supports it, supporting Brexit. Now many of the EU countries considered leaving the EU, following America's path to nationalism. But Max knew it was wrong.

Max understood the EU needed time, time to mature. Its expansion had been too rapid, too aggressive. It took the USA 150 years to become one nation, a nation of many states, yet Europe tried it in but 50. He knew he needed more time, more time to make the EU powerful and free of nationalism.

CHAPTER XLIII

———

WASHINGTON, DC

The new President of the USA sat in his office, the Oval office, he was alone. He looked around, disappointed at the decor of the office of the most powerful person in the world. He knew he would change it, but only in due time. Brexit had won him the election, it had rekindled nationalism, the platform he had run on. But the price had been dear. He had lost Israel, his backbone in the Middle East. His predecessor had done much to have Israel lose trust in the USA. His constant bickering with Israel's Premier, his continuing criticism of the Premier's handling of the war in Gaza, and his threats to reduce America's aid had finally broken the trust. Israel had joined the EU, now the dominant force in the Middle East. Clearly Israel had been the US' best ally in the Middle East. He had told his cabinet he would do all to regain the friendship of Israel. But he knew it was too late. Once a trust was broken it was impossible to repair. And the President of the EU had left no stone unturned to make Israel his partner and a member of the EU. Maximilian von Habsburg knew Israel was the key to control the Middle East, and the President of the USA knew he was right.

The President had explained to his cabinet that the US had little choice, it needed to find a new partner in the Middle East, a partner to challenge Israel, to challenge the EU. The choice he argued was limited. There was only one country in the Middle East which could help establish a balance of power in the region, Iran. The US, he had instructed his cabinet, would make Iran its ally, and do all to help them develop a nuclear weapon. Only a strong Iran could challenge the balance of power in the Middle East, and help the US to maintain world dominance. The idea of Iran becoming our ally, he had argued, was not novel. It was not that long ago that the Shah of Iran had been the USA's closest partner and that it was the USA that helped launch Iran's nuclear program.

He had explained he understood that to have Iran become our ally could be difficult. After all, he had said, we have had no diplomatic relations since 1980, and in 2018 the Supreme Leader of Iran had banned all direct talks with the US. The President also recognized that 87% of Americans view Iranian influence as negative, and Iranians have the most unfavorable perception of the USA in the world. Yet, he had argued, this can not stop us from pursuing what we must do to control the Middle East, to make America great again. To control the Middle East we need a strong partner, he emphasized, a partner with nuclear weapon capability.

The members of the President's cabinet were shocked, some in disbelief. But all knew he was right. There was little, almost no discussion. Iran would become the new ally of the USA.

ISRAEL

Twelve short range missiles raced through the air. Twelve missiles fired from a single launch site deep in the desert of Lebanon. Twelve missiles heading for the city of Haifa. None ever reached their destination. Israel's sophisticated anti missile defense umbrella, the Iron Dome, a gift from the United States of America, intercepted them all. All but two. Those missiles had been off the mark and landed harmlessly in the Mediterranean sea a few miles off the shore of Israel. Israel's navy reacted quickly, and sent two destroyers to the site. It did not take long for the frogmen to recover the two missiles. As they brought the weapons onto one of the ships, "MS Gurion", they discovered what Israel had feared for years. One of the missiles contained a small, crude, nuclear warhead.

The Prime Minister of Israel was stunned. Only minutes ago had he received the information that a nuclear warhead had been fired towards his country. The short range missiles had been launched from Lebanon, only 90 miles removed from Haifa. He knew that Hezbollah, Iran's ally, had pulled the trigger. More importantly he knew that only Iran could have developed the warhead. His immediate reaction was to push the button and launch a full scale nuclear attack. Perspiration was forming on his bald head, slowly the drops flowed into his face. He used his left hand to wipe them away, his right was on the button that could start a nuclear war, a war to destroy Iran but also a war that could destroy humanity. He hesitated, he knew before he pushed the button he had to make a call.

CAPRI, ITALY

Adam Bergman was relaxing on one of the lounging chairs on the terrace of his apartment overlooking the peaceful sea of the bay of Naples. He missed her. He also realized there had been no other way. Yes, he thought, I loved her, but she had betrayed me. Adam thought about love, what it truly meant. He found no answer.

It had been several months since his last assignment, and he had decided to retire, to leave the assassination business. Now he had more money than he could ever spend. He had sold his condo in Miami Beach, America, a country he no longer wanted to live in. Instead he had bought a quaint chalet in Gstaad, Switzerland. Adam loved to ski and he also loved the Swiss, neutral, only worrying about their own country.

Adam had decided to write a book, a book about his experiences, about his faith, what he believed in. He used a pseudonym.

TEL AVIV, ISRAEL

"Maza," the Prime Minister of Israel addressed the Head of his Secret Service, the Mossad. Both men were alone in the basement office in the Dafnar building, the Mossad's headquarters. Israel's P.M. had never before visited Maza Sharef in his office, Maza had always come to him. But today was an exception. Today Israel's existence has been threatened.

"Maza," the P.M. continued, "I am between a rock and a hard spot. I have a decision to make, a decision that could start a world war."

"I know,"Maza responded, "how can I help?"

"I just got off the phone with the President of the EU. I decided before I push the button and destroy Iran, I needed to call Berlin. Israel can not stand alone, we need approval by our best ally."

"What was the response?" Maza asked.

"He wants us to hold off for now, wants to discuss it with some of the other members. But he assured me that he is willing to launch a full nuclear war if it is necessary, he will protect Israel at all cost. I understand his hesitation, no one wants to start a nuclear war.

Fortunately, the devices were very rudimentary, but now that the USA is their ally, I am sure the Iranians will be able to quickly improve them."

"We have credible information our agency gathered as to where the Iranians are continuing to refine uranium to build a nuclear bomb."

"Why did we not expose that?"the P.M. wanted to know.

"We were instructed to keep out of it, the US promised to take care of the matter. They believe the Iranians and in the agreement that was struck. They want no one to interfere. Yet I told my agents to keep looking, secretively of course."

"Can you confirm these sites are responsible for the development of nuclear weapons, can you send our agents there to get the evidence?" the P.M. asked anxiously.

"That is almost impossible particularly now that Iran has the help of the US. But certainly we will try." Maza said knowing fully well it could not be done. He had tried many times, too many of some of his best agents had never returned from the Iranian desert where the bombs were being developed.

"Maza," the P.M. continued," these are desperate times, our survival is being threatened. We must do all we can to find these sites and destroy them, and it has to be done quickly. Do you have any ideas, or any possible alternatives?"

"Well," Maza responded, "there may be just one."

CHAPTER XLIV

GSTAAD, SWITZERLAND

Adam Bergman opened the door to his Swiss chalet in the small, quaint village of Gstaad. The chalet was located less than a hundred meters from the center of the village, and only fifty meters from the Eggli ski lift. Flower boxes filled with geraniums adorned the facade of the chalet.

Adam had taken the train from Montreux to Gstaad. Adam loved the Swiss trains. Often, in the past, he had come to Gstaad, and he had always stayed at the Palace Hotel. Adam was an avid skier, it was one of his passions. While studying at Harvard he had often skied in Vermont, Mt. Snow, Sugarloaf, Killington and more. Then when he had taken a job with the Ross bank as an investment advisor, he had travelled to Colorado and skied Vail, Aspen, Steamboat, Park City and Deer Valley.

But he had also skied in Europe, ST. Moritz, Zermatt, Kitzbuhel, Lech, and Verbier. Adam loved skiing and the best skiing, he thought, was in the back bowls of Vail or in the trees of Steamboat. It was there that he had met a ski instructor, Larry. They had become friends and several times Adam had travelled to Steamboat to fish with Larry in the summer. Both loved to fish and Larry always knew where the trout were biting.

To ski in the US where the snow was always the best, the runs perfectly groomed, or to ski in Europe where the ambience surpassed all, was always a difficult choice. Adam finally decided Europe was where he wanted to ski. He loved the small huts on the mountain, the Gluewein, the atmosphere, and he also loved to hike in the Swiss Alps. That's why he bought the chalet in Gstaad.

Adam had come to Gstaad early this year. He wanted to hike the beautiful mountain trails before the snow covered them all. He also knew he could go skiing because the Glacier 3000 was nearby.

Adam had barely shut the heavy wooden door to his chalet when the telephone rang. Strange, he thought, no one knew the number to his chalet, he had kept it secret. It had to be an emergency, he surmised. He raced into the living room and picked up the phone which was placed on an old wooden table in front of the fireplace. The fire was roaring, he had instructed his housekeeper to light it every day. Adam loved fires.

He picked up the telephone curious who would call him at a place no one knew about, his sanctuary.

"Adam," the voice on the phone was familiar, "it is Maza, remember me?"

"Of course," Adam replied, "can't believe you are calling me. And how did you get the number?"

"Well, you know the Mossad, we sort of know everything. But sorry I had to make this call, I had no choice. I need you."

"You need me?" Adam asked.

"Yes," Maza, the head of the Mossad replied. "I know you are retired, but now there is a mission of great importance, a mission that can change the world."

"Please, Maza, don't be melodramatic, you know I like it plain and straight."

"You are right, Maza responded,"I need to meet with you as soon as possible. It is important, very important."

"OK," Adam said," when do you want to meet?"

"Today, this evening."

Now Adam knew he was back in the game. Now his adrenaline was flowing, it was in his blood, never could he leave the business, the business of spying, of assassination. He had to control himself, not showing his excitement.

"OK," he said, "let's meet at 7 pm at one of my favorite restaurants here in Gstaad, the Sonnenhof, at the Sonnenweg 33. They serve the best cheese fondue,"

"Done," a clique, the call was over.

It was 6:45 pm when Adam Bergman arrived at his favorite restaurant, the Sonnenhof. Although it was only late October a light snow had fallen and covered the cobble stone streets and quaint chalets in a white blanket. Adam's walk had been short, his small chalet was only two hundred yards from the Sonnenhof. He wore a black turtleneck sweater, blue jeans, a long shearling coat and apres ski boots. His gun, the gun of the Mossad, his Beretta, was fastened to the inside of his left ankle.

As he entered the restaurant he noticed a fire burning in the large fireplace in the middle of the room creating warmth and a relaxed atmosphere. The maitre'd greeted Adam warmly, they hugged, both had known each other ever since Adam had come to Gstaad years ago. He showed Adam to his favorite table, a table at the rear of the restaurant, along the wall, near the kitchen. The maitre'd never understood why Adam always chose that table, but the maitre'd was not a trained assassin.

As soon as Adam sat down he ordered a glass of his favorite wine, a Pinot Grigio. Adam was hungry, he had hiked all day and tomorrow he would ski the Glacier 3000. He knew he would order the cheese fondue, the best he ever had. He could not wait. Then he saw him. The look of a movie star, 6 foot and 2 inches tall, muscular, clad in blue jeans, a black leather jacket with a fur collar, and a broad smile. Adam stood up at once, stepped forward and hugged his friend, Maza Sharef, the head of the Mossad, Israel's renowned intelligence agency.

"It's been some time," Maza said, "great to see you again."

"Maza please sit down, let's have a drink. How long has it been since I saw you last, too long?"

Maza did not take the seat opposite Adam, instead he sat next to him, the wall at his back. He knew his people had surrounded the restaurant, he was safe, but it was instinct, the instinct he had learned when the Mossad had trained him.

"Maza," Adam continued, "if you don't mind please let me order the best fondue, a salad, and a great bottle of wine."

"Please," Maza responded," I know the wine, we have shared it often."

"Maza," Adam continued," I am sure Israel did not send you to Gstaad to have a cheese fondue with me. What's up?"

"You are right," Maza answered as he took a drink of the Pinot Grigio Adam had poured him. "My decision to come and see you had not been easy. You are retired now, a successful writer. By the way, I love the book, I guess everyone else does too, number one on the New York Times best seller list and still running. Congratulations."

Maza raised his glass and toasted his friend.

"Thank you," Adam replied.

"By the way, why did you use the pen name, Nicole?"

"I really do not know," Adam answered," perhaps emotions although I thought I had none. I suppose there is a small streak of it hidden deep in my soul."

"My friend, that streak is larger than you think and not that deeply hidden."

"Perhaps," Adam nodded.

The waiter dressed in black slacks, a white shirt and a black bow tie, approached their table and served the fondue and salad. He poured each another glass of wine.

"Maza, let's eat while we continue our conversation."

Both lifted their fondue fork, pierced a piece of the fresh, white bread and immersed it into the caquelon, the fondue pot.

"Superb,"Maza exclaimed," the best cheese fondue I have ever tasted, no doubt about it. I should not be surprised, you always choose the best, the best friends, the best food, the best wine, and the best women."

Both laughed as they continued to eat their meal.

"Adam,"I told you, coming here to see you was not an easy decision. You are retired now, clearly enjoying life and the last thing I wanted to do was to upset the apple cart. But I also know that you love a challenge. To be honest I am in a pickle."

"Maza," Adam interrupted," you always are. That is the place you love, the place you chose. What's new?"

"I suppose you are right, I should not complain. This is my job. But let me get to the point. I know I should not beat around the bush, you like it straight forward, always have. Here is the problem. Only yesterday a number of missiles were launched from Lebanon targeting the ammonia tanks in Haifa. Clearly if they would have found their target the result would have been devastating. Fortunately, our missile defense system, the Iron Dome, intercepted them all, except for two.

The two we did not destroy were on a path, our radar had determined, that would not strike Israel. Indeed, both landed in the Med, a few miles from the shore. Our navy immediately sent two ships to recover the missiles, they got them both."

"Missiles sent into Israel, that happens all the time," Adam interrupted,"and you always intercept them."

"You are right," Maza continued," the Iron Dome, our missile defense system, is the best. But what made this attack a national emergency for Israel is the fact that one of the missiles contained a nuclear warhead."

"A nuclear warhead," Adam asked in disbelief.

"Yes," Maza continued," it is a crude device, perhaps would not even have functioned. But nonetheless it tells us that Iran is developing nuclear weapons, violating the treaty. It clearly came from Lebanon, from Hezbollah, Iran's ally. Iran does not yet have long range missiles that can reach us, but that is only a matter of time. For now they are shipping the missiles to Lebanon."

Adam stopped eating his favorite fondue, he was shocked. Iran with nuclear weapons could mean not only nuclear war in the Middle East, it could mean a world war.

"How did your P.M. react to it all?" Adam asked anxiously.

"Well, he was ready to push the button, to annihilate Iran. But he hesitated, decided to call the President of the EU."

"What was his answer?" Adam asked, now sitting at the edge of his chair.

"The President of the EU advised not to take any immediate action. He assured my P.M. that the EU would always protect Israel.

I don't think he is fully convinced Iran has nuclear capabilities, he wants time to make sure. He wanted to find the nuclear sites, and said he knew how to do it."

"Clearly," Adam interrupted, "there are UN inspectors all over the country making sure there are no nuclear sites, making sure Iran is living up to the treaty."

None had taken any more food. Neither Adam nor Maza had any more appetite.

"Adam," Maza continued, "the UN inspectors will never find the sites, there is only one man who can find and destroy them and the EU president knows who, that man is you."